Drift

Also by Leo Brent Robillard

Leaving Wyoming

Houdini's Shadow

Drift

a novel by
Leo Brent Robillard

TURNSTONE PRESS

Drift
copyright © Leo Brent Robillard 2011

Turnstone Press
Artspace Building
206-100 Arthur Street
Winnipeg, MB
R3B 1H3 Canada
www.TurnstonePress.com

Turnstone Press gratefully acknowledges the assistance of the Canada Council for the Arts, the Manitoba Arts Council, the Government of Canada through the Canada Book Fund, and the Province of Manitoba through the Book Publishing Tax Credit and the Book Publisher Marketing Assistance Program.

Although inspired by actual events, this novel is a work of fiction, and a product of the author's imagination.

Cover design: Jamis Paulson
Interor design: Sharon Caseburg
Printed and bound in Canada by Friesens for Turnstone Press.

Library and Archives Canada Cataloguing in Publication

Robillard, Leo Brent, 1973–
       Drift / Leo Brent Robillard.

ISBN 978-0-88801-385-9

       I. Title.

PS8635.O237D75 2011   C813'.6   C2011-903244-9

For Sébastien

Drift

De Aar

December 3 — December 6, 1899

1

*T*he young man stands facing north, where some miles away the first stirrings of a sandstorm erase the line of grimacing kopjes. The air is almost fluorescent beneath a cloudless sky, the way it has been since his arrival in South Africa. He knows that he should return to his newly erected tent, a bone-white sheet flapping one hundred yards behind him like a freshly laundered shirt, but he does not move. Within seconds, the first whirling, whipping grains of dust freckle his cheeks and hands, embed themselves in the khaki serge of his tunic. Their sting as sharp as little bees'. He shuts his eyes before he is overwhelmed completely. Sand in his nose, his hair. Sand filling the crack where his lips meet. Sand in his ears.

Will has never felt anything like it, not even a prairie snowstorm can match its pervasiveness. Will reaches for his handkerchief, then shakes it out and plasters it over his face. The sand is already caked in his lashes. He turns, stumbles, and then weaves a circuitous route back toward the tents, which are almost indistinguishable from the veldt now, awash in a rain of sand and dust. After only a few tentative yards, he is forced to lie down with his face in the earth. His lungs choke on the air. Prostrate, he crawls like a snake in the direction he believes the tents to be, pushing himself along on his elbows, swinging his hips—one hand securing the saturated cloth over his nose and mouth, the other reaching, testing, searching for the familiar texture of canvas. But in the end, it is the sound of canvas snapping that guides him, clear as a drumbeat.

In a momentary lull Will takes to his feet again, lunging head-long toward white. Pack mules bay in the distance. He is close now, he thinks, and then trips over a tether pegged in the ground, passing alongside his own tent. He is forced to forgo the handkerchief in order to negotiate the clasps affixing the flap, but when Will breaches the safe haven of the shelter, he falls on his knees and gulps air, bits of dust.

Robert looks up from his book, gazing at him over the wire rim of his spectacles through the half-light of the tent. Aware only now of the storm outside. Surprised by its vehemence.

‡

Both men are part of a Canadian contingent more than one thousand strong. They have answered the call from Mother England, gone to war again in some far-flung post of her empire. They have rallied to her cause—real or imagined. Some have arrived out of an antique sense of duty. Others, for reasons that are their own. Prairie boys, like Will. Journeymen without country, like Robert. And all points in between.

Even as they breathe the dirty air of the desert, both men are conscious that ships ply their way from ports in Melbourne and New Westminster, Liverpool and Bombay, en route for Cape Town and Durban—the last British footholds in South Africa.

Momentarily, history is confused. The Empire bewildered by the sudden turn of events. How could disparate bands of backward Dutch farmers have cowed the great armies of the world? Uneducated religious fanatics traipse the veldt in lord-like processions, while Britain scrambles, sloth-like.

‡

All day long Robert carves bits of soapstone into chessmen, beginning with the more difficult pieces of king and queen, and then descending through the ranks of bishop and knight. Rook and pawn. Will watches as Robert carefully files the rock into features, selecting the right tool from a small leather belt laid out beside him on the floor, and periodically holding the figures up to the light. Turning them over and over. These delicate anthropomorphisms.

Earlier, he asked Robert how he would create the opposing side.

"Quartz," the man answered without elaborating. It is the only conversation they have had since the storm began.

Will has soldiered with Robert almost two months and still knows next to nothing about him. He is a geologist, or at least he works with stone. This much, however, Will has gathered on his own. The man spends every free minute with his nose to the ground.

When he speaks, the accent is unmistakeably British, but why he is among A Company of the Winnipeg Rifles—the Little Green Devils —is a mystery. Mason claims he was in Canada with the Royal Geographic Society, but even that comes from a secondary source. The ring on his left hand suggests a wife.

Silence is the best armour, Will thinks, as he scrutinizes the man's craftsmanship, fine blue dust amassing like stalagmites beneath his big hands. And Robert wears silence like a cloak. Will knew a man like him back home in Portage la Prairie, an old Swede who lived in a tar-paper shack outside town. According to Will's uncle, the man owned half the arable land in the county, but he'd lost his wife to childbirth and remained a closed book thereafter.

He would come into their store once in a while like a stray dog, sniffing about. Sometimes he would need something to get by, but more often than not he would leave just as quickly as he had arrived, without a word to Will or his uncle. It used to give him the creeps, and he was glad to see him go.

Will doesn't have a choice about tenting with Robert, but if it weren't for the sandstorm, he would be out on the veldt with Mason.

Will is not sure what he expected from South Africa. He isn't even convinced that his decision to enlist was his own, and not some subversive manipulation of Mason, his childhood friend. He can remember his friend's disgust with the reports in the *Winnipeg Free Press* of Boer atrocities and injustices, and wishing to please him, Will can recall his own declarations. It is easier to agree with Mason than it is to dissent. He has the strength of his convictions. Will has only his vacillation, the product of a reflective mind unable to sink its teeth into anything resembling a belief, lest it prove, in the end, to be wrong. It is a characteristic learned or inherited from his uncle John, who until recently never expressed a definitive opinion on any subject. Will comes from a family that seeks the middle ground in all things, and perhaps this is why attaching himself to Mason is so attractive to him, if equally frightening at times.

When Robert finishes the last pawn, he lines them up as for a battle, then withdraws a lump of quartz from his kit and begins filing again.

‡

Inside the claustrophobia of his tent, Will attempts to write a letter to his uncle John, only the words do not come. He is hungry and the early pangs of dearth are already present in his stomach. The quartermaster was unable to start a cook fire during the storm, so it was biscuits and water for supper. Even the Kaffir hut is out of commission.

He did not see Mason outside the mess tent, but then they could not have spoken long in the blowing dust anyway. Robert, it seems, has fallen asleep, or he is feigning such to avoid the calamity of conversation. The rhythmic rise and fall of his chest is at odds with the random gusting beyond the tent walls.

The ambient light has all but disappeared, obliterated by the airborne sand, so Will lights a kerosene lamp to fend off the shadows. He has not written his uncle since he left, and finding a point to begin is increasingly difficult. How should he encapsulate the seven-thousand-mile journey over trackless ocean that has landed him here, among a regiment of dough-faced schoolboys in a distant British colony—a colony with unfamiliar place names like Bloemfontein, Naauwpoort, Kroonstad, and Klip Drift?

His initial memories of the voyage are already tainted with a quickly developing perspective of war. The whistle stops that ushered him along with the other recruits, full of people waving banners and flags, playing music, and passing milk plates of sandwiches up to the soldiers' extended hands seem part of another life now. The rainy silhouette of Quebec's ancient Citadel and its cobbled Old World streets melt under the blazing African sun, and his sea voyage aboard the *Sardinian* is swamped in sand.

I am swamped in sand, he writes, and then immediately tears it up. The next page bares its white teeth.

I live with a man who does not speak. He turns stone into flesh, little armies of men on horseback. My tent is a Bantu drum.

Will lifts the pen for a moment, considering.

Yesterday, we arrived in De Aar Junction, but I cannot see the town for sand. The kopjes are watching, I think. Did I mention we buried the first Canadian at sea? His coffin was a Union Jack. When we finally hit the indigo waters of the Gulf Stream, the men brought a pump and hose on deck. There were porpoises and flying fish.

We played through the battle of Nicholson's Nek.

The flame in the lamp flickers. Sand seeps in through the pores of the tent. Will writes.

I met her at the opera house in Cape Town. I think she kissed Mason. Her name is Claire.

‡

Sometime during the night the storm abates. He knows because he has not slept. The ensuing calm is like a dream he had once. The canvas walls of his tent collapse like emptied lungs. The roofline sags. And outside, he can hear the braying of the poor transport mules with nothing to drink but a trough of sand.

He has been trying to imagine the woman's face all night, but he can only remember her neck, the way she looked to him at the theatre from the next row back. The short locks of strawberry hair curled at her nape—anarchy reasserting itself in spite of the tight bun. The white nurse's cap. From time to time she would turn in response to something Mason said to her, and Will could trace the outline of her jaw, the slim aquiline nose, and impossibly fine ears.

He cannot imagine her tending to the wounded, her slim arms lifting and turning the bodies of men. Changing the beds beneath them, the filth of their chamber pots, or the festering state of their dressings. No matter how he looks at it, Will cannot associate her with the war at all. He views her instead as something above the war, something untainted by violence.

He has only just met her, but already she colonizes his thoughts. In the middle of the night, lost in the giant saucer of the Great Karoo, among thousands of men, she can find him like a stone tossed into water. The ripple.

‡

The next morning at breakfast, Mason is restless after a full day and night of inactivity. In De Aar they are stationed with the 2nd Battalion of the Duke of Cornwall's Light Infantry, and already this morning, he has been after their stories of the war. Stories that slip down the rail lines on the back of supply trains, or come overland with the Kaffir blacks.

The stories only cause Will to worry, but after Robert's silence even these are welcome.

"They're fighting not far from here, Will. At the Modder River," Mason manages to say between mouthfuls. "We should be there. Christ, Will, the bloody Boer will have packed up and left by the time we see action."

Physically, Will and Mason could not be more dissimilar. Mason is built like a boxer, broad-shouldered and tight. His hair is dark. His features small and quick. Will is the more slender of the two, with a slight edge in height. His hair is the colour of sand, like the veldt around him.

Mason asks, "Did you see the hotel in town where the officers slept?"

"No." Will finishes his second cup of coffee and wipes his mouth against his sleeve. The hunger he felt through the night is gone now.

"Only the best for our commanders, I say," Mason smirks. "I'm going to get a lay of the land after breakfast. You want to join me?"

"They've posted pickets and guards all over the camp," Will says by way of answering.

"They're not about to shoot a soldier for stretching his legs."

"No, I guess not."

"Why so glum?" Mason teases. "You still thinking of that Aussie nurse?"

A flicker of apprehension passes over Will's face.

"What?" he asks.

"That girl. What was her name?" Mason closes his eyes in feigned concentration. "Hilde. Wasn't that it?"

"Oh, right," answers Will. But of course he hasn't thought of Hilde at all. He has forgotten her completely, in fact. The woman who was beside him at the theatre, when all he wanted was to be with the one in front of him.

‡

After the close quarters of the *Sardinian*, Cape Town—spread out like a Turkish carpet at the foot of Table Mountain—was a revelation. Will stood on the deck with Mason as the transports for the Queenslanders and the Gordon Highlanders both cheered the Royal Canadians into harbour. Further along, by way of welcome, the brass band on the *R.M.S. Dunvegan Castle* struck up a rendition of the "Maple Leaf Forever." Hordes of citizens crowded the docks, tossing cigarettes and chocolate up to the soldiers who were leaning out over the railings.

Mason called out, "Did you save any of the fighting for us?" But his question was swallowed in the din.

That night, Will was too frantic to sleep. The troops had been ordered to spend one last night on board as their equipment was disembarked by a series of black boys clamouring for pennies. Will did his best to listen to his friend's excited banter, but soon his mind began to drift.

He awakened the next morning to the sound of a reveille, and hard upon troops were parading down the gangplanks and along Adderly Street all the way to Green Point Common, their first camp.

That night, both men were given free passes to the city and were pulled along by the throngs of evening traffic. The shops and factories had emptied, and labourers and clerks alike flooded the streets.

Will could not ignore the exotic tints of skin as he brushed past gaudily dressed Malaysians, Bantu-speaking blacks, and coloured, native-born Cape Towners. The wide stone-paved thoroughfares of Uppertown were crowded with hansoms for hire, private carriages, and legions of pedestrians. Hawkers and restaurateurs called to the passing soldiers. Bells rang in front of the newspaper offices, announcing the latest war bulletins, and the constant clang of the streetcars rose above the pandemonium as the open-air buses clattered past the smart-looking stone buildings with hopeful neoclassical facades, and white-washed native cottages capped with terracotta tiles.

Mason had them follow a troop of Aussies to a bowery show, but the girls only made Will blush, for which he was thoroughly razzed. Only later did they end up in a sample room for drinks.

It was Will who spotted her first, seated with a handful of other girls. All of them nurses stationed with the Queenslanders. But Mason, following the gaze of his companion's eyes, was the first to approach her. She stood out from the others with her red hair and opalescent skin, the slightly freckled nose. Mason had always maintained an easy way with girls. He never sat out a dance unless he chose to do so. And even there, halfway around the world in a foreign city amidst a nation at war, he could still find the right words to woo women.

The play at the Grand Opera House that night was a forgettable melodrama, but Will could not concentrate enough to afford it a fair chance. Mason and Claire whispered away the first act, while he sat dumbly staring, offering up one-word answers to the young woman beside him who was trying so desperately to engage him. Even during the intermission, when they sipped cocktails at marble-topped tables, Will could not help but drink in the other woman. The way she leaned in on one hand when listening to a conversation. Tossed her foot nervously when her legs were crossed. More than once she caught Will staring and smiled through her green eyes as though laughing at an inside joke.

But it was with Mason that Claire shared the hansom back to where she was billeted at the end of the evening, leaving Hilde and Will to suffer through their own excruciating cab ride in silence.

‡

De Aar Junction lies in the middle of a crater-shaped plateau surrounded by low-lying kopjes in the middle of the Great Karoo—a sparsely populated desert of low scrub, cactus, and thorn tree more than four thousand yards above the sea. To the north is the Orange River, and beyond that, the Kalahari. The Khoi-Khoi people, originally of the Table Bay area which is now Cape Town, were driven here by the Dutch settlers who attempted to enslave them. They eked out an existence in the Karoo and the Highveld by farming sheep and angora goats. But when the British arrived in Cape Town, the Dutch too decided to press north. The *trekboeren*, as they were called, clashed frequently with the black Bantu tribes as they fought over pasture lands.

Robert knows all of this before he arrives in De Aar. He read the right books on his passage over aboard the *Sardinian*, and picked up others while on leave in Cape Town. Now, as he walks through the sands east of De Aar Junction, he looks, however hopelessly, for remnants of these clashes, relics of tribal warfare. The ever-shifting sands and his lack of time render the search absurd, and yet it helps him pass the time between drills and parade—the only employment he and the other Canadians have had since their arrival a week earlier.

Unlike the younger men—boys, he is tempted to call them—this inactivity suits him just as well. Robert did not come here to fight. He came to escape the failure of his previous life: his research on prehistoric petroglyphs in the Milk River Valley north of Montana, his impending bankruptcy, and his wife, Veccha. Robert is happiest as he is now, alone and searching, although for a time he thought of himself as quite happy in the western frontier of Canada. There was enough artwork in the Milk River Coulee to devote a life to, and of course, there was Veccha. But he couldn't help but think that somehow in marrying her, he had interrupted something important—that his presence was an intrusion to her, to history. He had not expected to find a wife when he left England. His work in Australia at Ayers Rock had been more than successful. The Milk River petroglyphs were to be his crowning achievement as a scientist. But when he met her there on the prairie she seemed just as incongruous as he. It was only afterward that he understood the differences between them.

Veccha has a solidity that attracted Robert in the beginning, an earthiness that he lacks. Physically, she is voluptuous, like the women in paintings by Rubens or Renoir. She exudes a feminine strength that comes from her belief in intuition, a belief that Robert found quaint, initially, even tribal. It appealed to the anthropologist in him.

But he realizes now that he was too easily dismissive of her, in part because he could not measure or quantify what she knew or pretended to know. He is a scientist, after all. However, it is more than that. He is frightened by her impossible knowledge and self-possession. They rattle him.

More than a small piece of him began to believe in the things she told him and the others who sought her advice. And so he is in South Africa now, perhaps to flout the fate she presented to him. Or maybe he is here to simply fulfill the destiny she predicted.

In any case, Robert had all but exhausted the grant money from the Royal Geographical Society. He does not pretend that he had no other choice. He chose to leave.

He chose South Africa.

‡

There is a newspaperman travelling among the troops. A war correspondent from *The Globe*. Will noticed him on the *Sardinian*, always nosing about. But this is the first time he has actually spoken to the man. He's staying at a small hotel in De Aar Junction, billeted with the regimental officers. This, Will thinks, is his first foray into the desert heat. A chance to rub elbows, perhaps. Slum it with the men. He must, after all, be on the lookout for a story, something to feed the papers back home.

One afternoon, the man separates Will from the crowd. "I say, old boy, where are you from?"

The first thing that Will notices is the accent—faked, surely— more British than the British. He knew a widow back in Portage who was the same. An Anglophile, his uncle called her. Drank her tea from English china. Flew the Union Jack from her front stoop.

"Portage," answers Will. He's been detailed to unload supplies from a boxcar at the rail siding, and feels trapped.

"All this way for Queen and country, then?"

Will is hard-pressed to imagine a snout more ruined from drink. Thick and bulbous, the newsman's nose is shot through with tracks of broken veins. Hair protrudes from the nostrils, matching the stray white tufts above his ears. Hatless, thinks Will. He'll feel that later. Already his dome is a crisp red sheen.

Before Will can respond, the journalist rushes on. "Barrett," he says, offering his soft hand. "Mackenzie Barrett."

The man, sweating indecently in a three-piece suit, with his tie undone and collar wrinkled, looks around then, as though he is lost. Will stands politely.

"I say," he begins, finally. "Wouldn't have a spare shilling or two, would you?"

"Pardon?"

Barrett pats himself down as though searching for a key or a lost pair of glasses. "I sent a cable off. But, of course, the money's a bit late in arriving, you see."

Inhaling the sweet stench of liquor drifting from the newsman, Will raises his eyebrows.

"I'd see it gets back to you, of course."

"Of course," says Will, digging into his pants. At fifty cents a day, his pockets are rarely full.

"You're a brave lad," says Barrett eyeing the coin like a life preserver. "Such a fine bunch. Never seen the like."

Yes, thinks Will, as the man toddles off towards the hotel, for Queen and country.

‡

The train ride to De Aar had been as beautiful as it was exhausting, but Will had barely acknowledged the passing landscape. For almost two full days, forty-eight hours, the train plodded steadily north, climbing the high desert plateau. Outside Cape Town, it ran through large tracts of wheat fields and genuine farm country, not unlike the sights of Will's home province and his train passage through it little more than a month previous. However, beyond them, the land grew quickly barren with sparse vegetation and little population. The locomotive barrelled past a smattering of tribal villages, which were scarcely more than a collection of huts. But just before dark, the deep red globe of the sun softened the panorama, bathing everything in an almost ultra-violet hue, erasing the edges and transforming the vista into something more sublime.

The men, including Will, were tired after the previous night's leave in Cape Town and the morning's early rise and unexpected departure. Most were quiet if not sleeping as the train slipped into night. Several small groups gathered for a game of cards, but even these attempts did not last. Before long the train was a travelling tomb as it shuttled through the dark, and Will imagined himself the only man aboard still awake and dreaming.

Worcester. Matjiesfontein. Three Sisters. Biesjes Bull. Grasberg. Victoria Road. Richmond Road. Deelfontein and Mynfontein. The train stopped briefly at each one as it climbed throughout the next day. And when Will was not speaking with Mason, he was thinking of Claire.

‡

Campbell Scott arrives at the Canadian encampment like the lead float in a Christmas Day parade. Will is running a reconnaissance drill with Mason and the rest of A Company when the regiment of Royal Engineers arrives behind a team of twelve oxen pulling a hydrogen balloon—a great dark globe captured beneath a rubber web. The group is flanked by a unit of cavalrymen and several other supply carts bring up the rear. The last of which is a Kaffir hut pulled by two mules and driven by a black woman.

Even Lieutenants Blanchard and Hodgins cannot fault the men for stopping dead in their tracks. Both officers stare equally unabashedly at the carnival-like scene. The man aboard the lead cart, driving the extended team, is dressed in suspenders and a white collarless shirt, open clear down to a sizeable belly. His face is covered in several days' worth of salt and pepper growth, and his head is crowned in a sombrero cap, not unlike the cowpokes' back home. The man's flesh is tanned a deep red and fortified by layers of dark soil, no doubt kicked up by winds on the Highveld.

Rather than salute, the driver offers the men of the Little Green Devils a wave that ends with the tip of his hat.

"If that don't beat all," says a corporal named Hardy, who happens to tent with Mason.

When the order to fall in finally comes from Lieutenant Blanchard, the men are quick to respond and eager to follow the parade back to camp.

‡

Robert notices the balloonist from a long way off. His head, as usual, is not in the drill. Each time he carries his Lee-Enfield rifle, he cannot help but think how ridiculous he must seem to the others. His hands were not built to cradle a weapon. The sun on the veldt is pyrotechnic in the late afternoon, and he is sweating profusely in the khaki serge uniform. His glasses slip continuously off the edge of his nose and each time he has to push them back into place.

It is during one such manoeuvre that he notices the balloon undulating in the heat waves on the southern horizon. He is tempted at first to sound the alarm, but it is highly unlikely that the Boer will be approaching from that direction, marching boldly across the open plateau. It isn't until some time has passed that he realizes just what the object is, and shortly thereafter, the rest of the company picks up on its presence as well.

He tries to imagine how he will describe its appearance to Veccha. He has written her a letter each day since he left, though he has sent none of them. Not when the *Sardinian* passed the England-bound *Rangatira* at sea, not when he reached Cape Town. Nonetheless, he continues to write them, if only as a way to process his involvement in the war.

Veccha would tell him that the balloonist is an omen, he thinks. She would see it as a sign. And not for the first time, he just might believe her.

‡

The quartermaster is already doling out dinner when Will returns from the reconnaissance drill. The arrival of the balloonist is on everyone's lips. Will learns from a private in G Company that the Royal Engineers are putting a road through the kopjes to the north to aid the passage of Howitzers and nine-pounders. The rail lines are being constantly sabotaged and raided by Boer marauders. At Kroonstad, the tracks are peeled up like the beached skeleton of a whale, so the military needs a reliable road for the horse carts to pass. Only that does not explain the balloonist.

Will catches Mason on his way to the mess. "Do you want to check out the balloon?"

Mason shrugs. "Maybe after dinner."

"Let's grab something from the Kaffir hut," Will counters. But Mason just makes a face.

"Oh, come on."

Reluctantly, Mason turns back and accompanies him in the direction of the Royal Engineers. The balloon is difficult to miss. It is the only structure of any height on the plateau, rising perhaps twenty yards from the veldt floor. It is spherical with a tapered teat dangling toward the basket and the tanks where hydrogen is stored. The entire structure is covered in webbing, and a ring of metal cord encircles the bottom third of the sphere. To this a series of ropes is attached which secure the balloon to the basket.

The balloonist is at the Kaffir hut himself, eating from a plate of prepared food.

"Good afternoon," Will salutes.

The man looks up from his food and withdraws a red handkerchief from his back pocket to mop his face.

"This your balloon?" Will continues.

"It was," answers the balloonist.

"I'm Private Will Regan and this is Private Mason Black," offers Will.

"Campbell Scott," says the man, no rank included.

"What do you mean by 'was'?" asks Mason.

"Let's just say the British can be persuasive when they want something," Campbell responds. His accent is like that of the coloured Cape Towners—not quite British, not quite Afrikaans.

Will asks, "You're not a military man?"

Campbell laughs. "I told them if they wanted the balloon, they had to take the driver with it. Warts and all. I guess you could say I'm a man for hire."

"Hired for what, exactly?" asks Mason, examining the balloon more closely.

"Reconnaissance," he says. "I fly over the Boer trenches, report back to the British."

"They don't shoot you down?" Will inquires.

"I try and stay out of range. Besides, it would take fifty or sixty shell holes before the ballast was affected."

Mason points at the plate of food. "That stuff any good?"

"Why don't you give it a try?" he responds. "Have a beer to wash it down."

"Beer?" says Will.

Campbell smiles and then says something to the black woman in the hut in an unintelligible tongue. A few moments later a boy arrives with two more wooden plates. His little black belly sticks out over dark red linen pants. His feet are bare.

Will nods his thanks and pays the lad. The food is slightly spicy and consists of dried meat and unidentifiable vegetables, maybe roots.

"Not bad," says Mason. "How about that beer?"

When the child returns, he has two goblets of a rather ill-smelling purple beverage. Will sniffs it hesitantly, and then takes a sip.

Campbell smiles at the look on the soldier's face as he attempts to keep it down.

"An acquired taste, for sure," laughs Campbell.

Mason sets his aside.

"It'll put hair on the balls of your feet."

The black woman is smiling from the hut, working over a cutting board. She does not look up, but Will can see that she has a handsome face. High cheekbones. Smooth dark skin.

Will turns away from the woman. "Would you take me up sometime?"

Campbell cleans his mouth with two fingers. Smooths his scrawny moustache. "You'd be interested, then?" he says, sucking his teeth.

Will nods.

"Not me," says Mason.

The balloonist pats his belly. "There's a writer that's been after the same thing. Bit of a nose on him."

"Barrett," says Will.

Mason looks at him, raises a single brow.

"Yes. You've met, I take it."

"He was a bit short on cash."

Campbell laughs. "A borrower nor a lender be," he says. Then he barks something over his shoulder to the woman. She clucks, but does not respond.

"We'll see what we can work out, young William. We shall see."

‡

Hardy holds court the next morning in front of Mason's tent. Will's tent mate rarely speaks, but Mason's more than compensates. Hardy is a corporal, promoted because of his experience with the Northwest Mounted Police. He talks often and to anyone who will listen about his exploits in the '85 rebellion or the Yukon gold rush in the north, but Will suspects the Mounties stuck him somewhere quiet and remote—a suspicion supported by the man's girth.

Usually Will likes to pick up Mason and escape whatever tale the man is weaving. However, this morning Hardy is not discussing his favourite topic. It is the balloonist instead to whom he turns his attention, so Will slows up and joins the small crowd of gossipers.

"Being a cavalryman myself, I was simply discussing the merits of revolvers and the Mexican loop holster favoured by our Canadian Mounted Rifles, when the conversation turned to our man Campbell Scott," prattles Hardy. "Seems he gave the British military a hard time when they came to commandeer his balloon for the service."

"What sort of hard time?" asks a private unknown to Will.

At that same moment, Mason emerges from the tent, straightening his tunic.

"Seems he refused entirely at first, even went so far as to draw a gun on the inquiring major and his troops."

"Campbell?" inquires Mason.

"None other," continues Hardy, shifting his weight. "And that's not all," he says, dangling the information like a carrot.

"Go on with it," Mason shoots.

Hardy eyes Mason as though he is considering pulling rank, but returns to the story instead. "Seems that Kaffir woman isn't just any old woman," says Hardy.

"What's that supposed to mean?" asks Will.

"Means that darkie is his wife." Hardy leans back, rocking on the balls of his feet.

"Get out," sniffs Mason.

"Whose children do you think are running around over there?" asks Hardy, cocking an eyebrow.

"The boy?" asks Will.

"The boy. The girl. There's at least half a dozen of them."

Mason snorts but doesn't refute it.

"How can a white man sleep with that savage?" asks the earlier private, and several others nod.

"Oh," says Hardy. "Campbell isn't white." Hardy smiles as though he just delivered a *coup de grâce*.

"So," says Will, deflating the moment and stealing Hardy's thunder. "I mean, so what if Campbell's coloured and his wife is black?" Will can feel something building inside him as he speaks, and Hardy can see it. Will can tell by the fat man's reaction.

"I was just saying what I heard," stammers Hardy, not wanting to make the point any more clear.

"Then you weren't really saying anything, I guess." And with that, Will spins on his heel and walks off in Campbell's direction. And in an unrealized moment of reversal, Mason follows.

‡

Mason and Will have been friends since childhood. They had both graduated high school together the year before the war broke out. Mason went to work as a typesetter for his father's newspaper, and Will began to work full time at his uncle John's grocery store, ostensibly saving for college in Winnipeg. He and Mason had often talked about leaving, but each of them was attached to Portage in his own way. Will had his uncle, the man who had raised him from childhood. And Mason was the Golden Boy. The athlete. The one everybody loved, except Will's uncle John.

Mason made the old man nervous with his talk of moving to the city, setting out on an adventure. John Regan was a quiet man with a small, but happy life. He wanted the same for Will, though he was more than willing to acquiesce to college if that was what the boy truly wanted, and as long as he came back afterward. John viewed it more like a sowing of wild oats than a furtherance of education.

So when the two friends burst into his store one Saturday afternoon, wearing ridiculous local militia outfits and explaining that they had volunteered, John removed his apron slowly.

"I have never looked upon two more foolish boys," he said, staring them down for what seemed like a very long time to Will. And then he left through the front door without closing up shop.

His uncle, the perennial diplomat, had never expressed himself in such certain terms.

‡

Like a view from the *Sardinian* on a clear day, the world tilts away from the bucket of Campbell's balloon. It's the reason early sailors suspected that the earth was round. From this height, the observation is unmistakable. Will feels the bottom of his stomach fall out as they rise. Campbell plays with the hydrogen valve, and Barrett pukes.

"Bugger me," Campbell says without enthusiasm.

"Bloody sorry, old boy," offers the journalist. "Touch of motion sickness, what?" Most of the liquid clears the wicker basket. Some does not. A chunk of something orange decorates the ledge of the bucket, suggesting that at some point Barrett actually consumed solids. The air is rank in the balloon.

"You're stinking," observes Campbell, otherwise nonplussed.

"I do believe you've hit the proverbial nail, chappy."

Will considers the fate of the unfortunate engineers milling below.

"Used to do this for a living," says Campbell, settling down.

"What's that?" says Will.

"At fairs and carnivals, like."

"In South Africa?"

"No, no," Campbell says dismissively. "I lived in England for a time."

Will grows more daring now that the device has levelled off, tethered to the earth below, and no longer rising. He approaches the edge, taking the ledge of the bucket in both hands, leaning out. The desert stretches toward the horizon in all directions, interrupted only by low blue hills and tracks of green scrub. A scar of railway line disappears into the northeast haze.

"Beautiful, isn't it?" says Campbell.

"Funny," interjects Barrett. "I never pegged you for a Romantic, Scott." The correspondent has developed a habit of using family names as a form of intimacy. Goes with the accent, thinks Will.

"A realist, sir. Please," says the balloonist. "It is beautiful on the surface. From this height."

Barrett still appears a little green, and pursues the conversation no further.

"What's beneath the surface?" asks Will, turning from the view.

"Ha. Don't get me started." Campbell fiddles with the hydrogen valve. It is amazing how little it takes to change the orb's altitude. "What about you? What brings you to the Dark Continent?"

It's the second time the question has been asked of him. Both men who did the asking are in the bucket. Will can only shrug, though, and with luck, dismiss the inquiry.

"What? Not here for honour, then? Glory?"

Will returns to the sea of sand, spreading green and hot yellow beneath them.

"Adventure?" Campbell presses.

"Perhaps," he acquiesces.

"Well, that's something I know a thing or two about."

"Sorry, but ..." says Barrett, "... think I'll just have a wee snooze over here. If it's not too much of a bother." Campbell watches the man curling into a corner of the basket.

"A regular Alan Quartermain, what?"

Will smiles.

Campbell returns to his controls. "Nothing wrong with a little adventure, Will."

Only Will isn't sure if the balloonist means something else altogether, and decides to press him further. "You don't agree with the war, then?"

"Perhaps the war doesn't agree with me," Campbell smiles. "How does a war agree with someone, anyhow?"

Will blushes.

Campbell persists. "Does it agree with you?"

At that moment, Barrett begins to snore. Will looks from Campbell to the newsman and then back over the earth. "I guess I haven't seen much of it yet," he answers. "Other than marches through the desert."

"Count yourself lucky, then," says Campbell. "I don't want to fill your head with platitudes, boy. I'm not going to say war's hell. That's just what it is," Campbell scoffs. "I guess you've come a long way to learn so little."

"I suppose I'm not really clear what it is we're supposed to do," stammers Will. "I mean, back home the papers ... and Mason ..."

"Black and white," says Campbell, not without irony, and then relents. "This isn't the first war in Africa. And it will not be the last. Africa is a rich man's playground. And every playground has its bullies. But you won't find that in your papers." Campbell nods in Barrett's direction and then moves to the edge of the basket with Will.

"There are European footprints all over this continent. But the wind erases them eventually."

‡

Will watches him out on the veldt. His head is bent to the ground, searching. For what, Will wonders. Robert has not left the area for at least fifteen minutes. Every so often he bends, brushes away sand, scoops the earth into his hands and throws it away. On his haunches, and from a distance, he looks like primitive man, last of the Great Apes.

Will sits in the dust no more than one hundred yards from the tent line, legs spread before him, knees up. He has amassed a collection of small stones, debris from the veldt, and now and again he tosses one out to the desert. The sky is an azure bowl above him. For a while, Mason crouched close by, carrying a one-man conversation. Trying to fill the absence created by his friend's silence.

"The Cornwalls say the Boer are watching us from those kopjes to the northeast," he had said. "Looking to raid the supply trains as they pass through the hills." But Will wasn't biting.

He is surprised with his own reaction to Hardy's aspersions. Why should he have jumped to Campbell's defence? Why does he think that Campbell needs defending? Does Will not think it odd for a white-coloured man to be living among the Bantu tribes? Perhaps it's the waiting that has made him touchy. The days of anticipating something, anything to happen. Or maybe he wants the war to be about ideals, to mean more than diamonds and gold, as he fears it boils down to. The Boer keep slaves. The British do not. Isn't that it? Isn't that worth fighting for? Or perhaps Will is comforted that someone like Campbell is involved in the war at all. Reassured that his own convictions are not misplaced. From the balloon, however, Will has already learnt a lesson in perspective.

Robert moves suddenly in the distance, crouching forward, knuckles on the ground. Will tosses a stone. The figure on the veldt rises to full height, and suddenly ape becomes man holding his find to the light of the sun. And although Will cannot be sure from this range, he believes that Robert is smiling.

‡

The balloonist stumbles back to the hut where his family sleeps like stones. The night is close and moonless. He is a little drunk, but not shellacked. Nonetheless, he doesn't want to wake his wife, face her wrath. Disappointment. If not for him, she'd be safe at home now. Not toddling after a white army, feeding off it to get by.

Of course, she could have gone back to her family. Taken all Campbell's cattle. Paid her own way, and that of their children. But she wouldn't do that to him, to herself. There's more pride in what she's doing now, he thinks. Or at least, she'd see it that way.

Barrett's ship came in. Or rather, his wire did. Otherwise, Campbell would have been back hours ago. Instead, he reeks of Scotch and has trouble walking straight.

The fat man stops outside the wagon and listens for sounds of life—hears nothing—and proceeds to undo the flap of his trousers, urinating in an arc over the desert floor, spilling some over his hands in the process.

"Bugger me," he curses.

Barrett or not, he'd have managed a good sousing either way, he finally admits. It's a way of forgetting. About the war. About his gypsy existence. The past is like an unlocked door, blowing open in all weather.

He thought himself through with war, for instance. With the world of white men parading through deserts. He was bullocks as a farmer. His wife's father told him as much. But he was getting partial to being bullocks. Stationary bullocks.

Adventure, in spite of what he told Will, is not all it's cracked up to be. A good woman, he thinks. With an ample backside. Kids. Enough to trip over. That's the thing.

"Leave adventure to the lads," he says aloud, doing himself up. The Milky Way is a swath above him. "I'm too old for this."

And then he is flat on his ass.

‡

Finally, after days of inactivity, the order to bivouac arrives. The troops are moving seventy-five miles north to Orange River. Campbell and the engineers are to accompany them by train. A transport arrives the following morning and the man's balloon is collapsed and stored on a special rail car amid much cursing and swearing. Will is glad to know that he will have more time to talk to the enigmatic balloonist.

However, as the Canadians are taking possession of their rail accommodations, Will hears an argument break out at the railway junction. Campbell is exchanging words with an officer of the Duke of Cornwalls. A young and blushing lieutenant. Will and Mason both fight for a place at the window as the troops lean out to investigate the hubbub.

"Sir, this is a military transport, not a passenger train," says the lieutenant, aware of the audience and trying to stop his voice from breaking.

Campbell says something in a language Will cannot understand, a language different from the one he used with the Kaffir woman, and then to the shock of all those watching, he spits in the earth by the officer's boots. Before the argument can progress, an older lanky major with a handlebar moustache interrupts them.

"Baggs, my good fellow, surely we can find space for a few more," he says in a good-natured tone. "Come out of the sun, and we'll see what can be arranged, shall we?"

Momentarily placated, Campbell accompanies the two men into the station.

The soldiers leave the windows only somewhat disappointed by the show of diplomacy, and continue stowing their gear.

Will hears Hardy across the aisle. "He won't leave the woman behind. Actually wants us to ferry the whole bloody family."

‡

After climbing through Houtkraal, Pontfontein, and Pauwpan, the train comes to a stop at Kraankuil. Will plays cards or listens to Mason speak wistfully of killing Boers for most of the trip, or stares out at the ostrich farms in an otherwise unchanging landscape. At one point, early on, a Cape Breton fiddler strikes up a jig for the men in the aisles, but eventually as the clock approaches noon, the temperature rises to a critical level, compounded for the men on the train by the black smoke vomited back from the engine, and the close quarters within. The problem becomes so acute that a general lethargy has settled over the troops as the locomotive finally hisses to a halt.

Will feels as though he is hit with a camera flash the moment he steps off the train. The heat is dizzying. By the platform, a group of soldiers huddles beneath the meagre shade of a few thorn trees. Laughter breaks from their ranks and Will slowly makes his way over to investigate.

At the centre of the storm is a handful of girls in traditional white sunbonnets. Each of them carries a pail of water and is ladling out drinks to the men. The laughter, Will discovers, arises from the soldiers' inability to communicate their appreciation. The girls blush and prattle on in a regional dialect the men cannot seem to crack. Campbell arrives at the same moment from the opposite direction and says something to the prettiest of the bunch that makes her giggle and turn away.

"Are they speaking Dutch?" asks Will, wiping the fresh water from his lips.

"Taal, actually. But yes, they are of Dutch descent," says Campbell. "Be sure to try the cakes if you can find them. A real delicacy," he adds, rubbing his sizeable belly. The smell off him is terrible.

Will presses the man further. "Shouldn't we be worried? Them being Dutch and all?"

Campbell pulls the dirty red handkerchief from its roost and mops his face. "Worried?" he chuckles. "Of poisoning, you mean? Not at all. They're farm girls, my boy. Not burgher spies."

"They're not Boer, then?"

"Boer? Do you even know what that means?" asks Campbell.

"It's Dutch," comes a disassociated voice, familiar and unfamiliar all at once. "For 'farmer.'"

Will turns to find Robert polishing his glasses.

"Isn't that so, Mr. Scott?" he says to Campbell.

"Exactly. Campbell, please."

Will isn't sure what should surprise him most, that Robert knew the answer, or that he volunteered the response. The paradoxical soldier extends the balloonist a hand once his glasses are firmly in place.

"This is the enemy," says Campbell, loud enough for those nearby to hear, and opening his arms to encompass those assembled.

Will must have a perplexed cast in his face, as Campbell continues, "You were expecting something a little more evil, I presume. I can only imagine the recruitment posters in the colonies." Campbell's mood changes suddenly as he squints up the line past the locomotive to the watery horizon. "No, my boy," he says more quietly. "This is it."

2

Orange River

December 7 — December 9, 1899

*T*here are women in Cape Town, down by the wharves, waiting in the cool mouths of doorways, breathing sultry promises into the ears of every passing soldier. Their bodies are the crossroads of nations. Their skin, the product of the Malay, the Javanese, the East Indian, and the Malagasy slave alongside her Caucasian slaver. Three hundred years of breeding. Coal skin and blue eyes. Fair-haired and bronze. These women offer up a history lesson in forced migration and imperial oppression, with hearts as cold as the Benguela Current and bodies hot as the south equatorial Agulhas.

Will has seen them with their lips rouged and pouting. Sniffed the exotic scent of them in alleys too dark to enter. He has heard they carry knives in their stockings, that they are prepared to cut the throats of their fair-weather lovers for money. It is not their war. It is not even their country. But they will feed from it. *Bring us your empire, your colonial sons,* they say, *and we will allow them their manifest destiny for sixty seconds and a handful of shillings.*

After only a month, Will is prepared to apologize for his ancestors. But these women are bored with repentance. They wait only for the next ship to come in. The siren call of a continent ripe for the picking.

‡

On his field map, Will can see that the Orange River originates in the mountains of the Grand Escarpment near Giant's Castle and plunges onto the plateau that constitutes the Great Karoo. From there, it wanders through the Boer territories of Kenhardt and Pruska, the Dutch burgs of Douglas and Hopetown, until it severs the government rail line north of the Orange River station. But what the map does not tell him is that the Orange River junction is a barren wasteland of dust, hotter than a blast furnace, baked by sun.

Several times the soldiers march to and from the train, disembarking their equipment for what promises to be a prolonged stay. The camp is a flurry of activity as the soldiers erect their temporary homes upon recently vacated ground. Will and Mason are given garbage detail and spend the better part of the afternoon staking detritus from the last regiment and filling canvas sacks with garbage that will be burned or buried the following day. The abandoned latrines produce an awful stench that induces retching in several of the privates nearby, and there is some worry from the medical officers about the spread of dysentery and enteric fever. Eventually, the order is given to dig new facilities, and a contingent of unlucky souls is assigned to fill in the preexisting dump. Long after his detail is over, Will sees the men, heads wrapped in towels and handkerchiefs, shovelling the pulverized sand back into the pits.

The site is close enough to the front that heavy guns and mortar fire can be heard like a periodic hammering in the distance throughout the day, and in spite of his disappointing detail, Mason is in good spirits because of it.

"A day or two and we'll be on that front line, Will," he boasts, staring off at an imagined vista.

Much later, an enterprising private from E Company rigs a length of frayed hose to a vacated pump and a horse trough of soupy water. Will and Mason both take advantage of the opportunity to shower for the first time since they crossed the equator. Although the trickle is a lukewarm bath, in this heat it is nonetheless a tempting draught. However, neither is willing to risk the rumoured fever.

Somewhat refreshed, the two retire to their respective tents. That same night, around midnight, the rains finally arrive.

‡

It is most definitely part of a musical instrument. And because he expected to find nothing, Robert is elated. He turns the piece over in his hand. Outside, the rains falls, a steady flush after weeks without water. The cylindrical shape suggests a flute of some sort. Clay, he suspects, or petrified wood. It is completely devoid of any ostentation, any decoration. And the piece in his possession retains only one borehole. A single note.

Even here there is music, Veccha, he writes as his opening line.

He remembers the music of the Australian Aboriginals, and wishes now he had paid more attention when he was there. Their polyrhythmic beats, the cyclical patterns repeated independently of one another, are probably quite like the Bantu music. Only here the drum is most likely the instrument of choice. He has read about the language of drums in Africa. The use of talking drums to communicate over vast distances. The same way the Aboriginals use the didjeridoo or the sling.

He had been encouraged by the discovery of the ruined Kaffir kraal. Of course there was no way of dating the stone foundation. The desert reclaims its dead quickly. But there was potential. He is sorry to have left the site so soon, but there are always possibilities with a river.

A river is full of possibility, he writes. It is another letter he is unlikely to send. This lack of communication is only an extension of his life with Veccha. Constantly they were unable to find the proper channel through which to pass.

Even in the evening heat of their cabin on the prairie, after sex—the closest they ever came to communing—they could never find the right words. And for this, Robert feels an acute sense of failure.

He has always felt more at ease with rocks and relics than he has with people. He can sense Will's desire to befriend him, for instance, and yet he doesn't know where to begin.

He notices a certain nobility in Will. Like Robert's wife, he continues to operate in a world where we are too often victims of forces beyond our control—and yet Will does not seem to despair. He seeks instead a way to understand, to come to grips with those forces.

Slowly Robert is beginning to understand that his decision to come to South Africa might be his own way to accept the inevitability of those same forces.

There is so much he could tell Will, if he could only find the words.

‡

The next morning, Will observes Mason kicking stones across the camp, a thundercloud above his head. He greets Will with a scowl.

"They're shipping the Gordons north to Magersfontein," he says, shaking his head. A half regiment of the Gordon Highlanders is camped nearby. Will noticed their kilted presence during the disembarking of the *Sardinian*, and there had been a piping of the last post late the night before.

Will stares blankly at his friend. "I'm sorry, Mason."

"You're sorry. Doesn't it make you angry?"

"Angry?"

"The waiting!" Mason takes him by both shoulders. "What's wrong with you, Will? Don't you want to fight?"

"I'm not sure anymore, Mason."

His friend's eyes open wide. "What are you saying? Do you want to go home and tell people in Portage that we went on a camping trip? This is our big chance."

"To do what?"

"To make a contribution. To be somebody, Will. To … to matter."

Will cannot think of how to answer him. To tell him that he isn't sure that the war is the right thing anymore. That he doesn't know what right is. In fact, he envies Mason's convictions, his ability to commit wholeheartedly, when he himself is in such a crisis of conscience.

Instead he says, "We'll get our chance, Mason. You have to be patient."

"Ahhh," Mason groans, and turns away. Will takes in the slant of his athletic build, like a runner stuck in the blocks. The faint popping of guns can be heard again, far off in another world.

‡

The order to build a railway siding and a landing goods platform comes as a surprise to the troops. They have become so used to drilling and parading and loafing that the proposal to create something is actually greeted with good humour. Two hundred men and five officers from the various companies are assembled by the track. Will and Mason among them. Hardy and Robert as well. Will is surprised to see Campbell standing with the volunteers, who lean shirtless in the rejuvenated sun awaiting orders.

All five acquaintances end up on the same detail with a handful of others. Their job is to lay track. With picks and shovels they set about the task with quiet determination. Will revels in the exertion, the bend and pull of muscles long out of use. Even at two men to a sleeper, the weight on their shoulders is tremendous. It takes four of their party to transport the iron rails. Before long the strike and ring of the two-pound sledges reverberates through the camp at a steady pace. The French Canadians in their crew send up a rendition of "L'arbre est dans ses feuilles" that makes the Anglophones laugh and applaud.

At lunch time, the men toss down their tools and sit in the shade of a thorn copse. Conversation wanders between them like water. Even Hardy is amused by the balloonist's stories.

Just before the bell sounds for a return to work, Will spies a line of approaching cavalry. As the slow-moving horsemen approach and crystallize out of the waves of heat, Mason recognizes them.

"The Lancers," he says with a sense of awe.

"The 16th Lancers," confirms Campbell, finishing a mouthful of sandwich.

The riders, dressed in dun-coloured gob caps and matching uniforms, sidle side-to-side as their slow-moving mounts parade silently past, the tell-tale lances like empty flagstaffs in their hands. No one waves or salutes them, nor do the horsemen make any salutation of their own. The long line of them looks only forward; the horses, at the ground. All conversation ceases as they pass, and even when they are gone, the men sit in respectful silence.

"Going up the Modder River," says Campbell at last, wiping the red handkerchief over his brow.

"Did you see those horses? Those uniforms?" says Mason. "Now that's a soldier."

Several others nod their agreement.

Campbell affixes the young man with a curious stare, picks at his teeth. Mason stares back.

"Antiques," Campbell says, finally.

"What?" says Mason, eyes narrowing.

"Antiques, I said. Relics. Don't envy them, boys. You've just been party to a death march." Campbell leans back against the hard trunk of a thorn tree. "You boys ever seen a Pom Pom gun in action? A Maxim-Nordenfeldt? Sixty rounds per minute, lads. A belt of twenty-five one-pound shells. You won't soon forget it, I can tell you. So don't envy them, I say. They won't get close enough to use those pretty javelins."

The men finish their lunch in a silence to match the passage of

Lancers. By the end of the day, the siding and the platform are complete, and a half-mile of track stretches into the desert.

Uncle John,

*Yesterday, rain fell out of a blue sky, and today we built a
railway to nowhere. South Africa is a land of contrast and
paradox. There is a man among us who has flown, and I
have seen birds condemned to walk the earth. Here, the
enemy feeds us cake, and the water is feared to be poisoned. I
have seen the living dead parading on horseback.*

*A soldier I met searches the sand for what we have lost.
I'm not sure, but I think he has found something. We are the
same, he and I. Only he is more successful. I fear that perhaps you were right after all when you called us fools. I have
not found what I was looking for. I'm not sure that I even
know what it was anymore, or that I ever did know.*

*How is the store? Have you noticed the creak in the
floorboards, behind the counter where my aunt Mary used
to stand? If I close my eyes I can almost believe that I am
among the shelves stocking cans again. Don't forget to order
cranberry sauce for Christmas. We forget that every year,
and Mrs. Jessup is an unforgiving woman.*

Do you think I should write to her? Claire, I mean.

Yours,
Will

‡

Will sits up in bed. Three, he thinks. He counted three shots in the
night. There is some confusion emanating from the British encampment where the Shropshires are stationed. Robert sleeps oblivious. In

a moment, Will is outside in only his trousers, bare feet on the sand and stone—oddly warm still, long after the sun has gone down. It is a short walk to the perimeter, and already a small crowd has gathered thirty yards beyond, in the desert. A cluster of lanterns, like nervous fireflies, beat back the African night. Several of those gathered are Canadians, but the majority are British soldiers speaking in hushed tones with some urgency.

When Will arrives, the problem is obvious. One of the Shropshire lads lies several yards off amid the stones in a pool of his own blood, body twisted, one leg beneath his back. His eyes are open and ghastly in the dark.

The British lieutenant is still tightening his belt when he joins the growing crowd. "Boer sniper?" he asks, incredulous.

"'Fraid not, sir," answers one of the privates, dressed as though on reconnaissance.

"How's that, private?" the officer demands.

"Drury shot him, sir," says the man. He points toward the tent line where a smaller group has gathered round a seated man. His face is cupped in his hands, and Will can just make out the heaving shoulders, the sobs.

"Bloody hell. How did he manage that?" One of the lieutenant's shirttails is loose at the back. Will has the sudden urge to tuck it in.

"Barton, sir—the deceased, if you will—would not respond to the perimeter guard, sir. When asked, sir. By Drury, sir. Barton was coming back from patrol."

"Bloody hell."

"So you said, sir."

‡

The funeral is as sombre an affair as Will has ever witnessed. Both camps, the Shropshires and the Royal Canadians, turn out in full to watch the parade. An impromptu military band plays the march, several Canadians among them. Those in the procession carry their rifles backward with bayonets fixed. Will cannot take his eyes off the coffin. Like that of the soldier they buried at sea, it is draped in the Union Jack. But the coffin itself is wheeled on a gun carriage. It bumps and shifts and slides as the cavalcade travels out to the makeshift grave. At one point the whole apparatus threatens to tip over, spilling its cargo unceremoniously before the gathering.

The British officers argued about the grave earlier that morning. It could not be dug the requisite six feet. The earth was too hard. Bedrock too near the surface. The hole, as observed by Will, was barely deep enough in which to set the coffin. After some debate, it was decided that stones be gathered and then set upon the grave so as to discourage scavengers. The troops had searched all morning for enough boulders of the right size, many travelling far into the desert and stumbling back a half-hour later under the weight of a single stone.

Will stands still throughout the entire procession, until the body is laid to rest and the first shovelfuls of earth are cast upon it. He does not see the soldier who mistakenly killed the unfortunate Shropshire at the service, but the accompanying volley, heard for miles around, must be a grim reminder no matter where he waits in the camp. When the buglers complete the "Last Post," the band begins a quickstep for the withdrawing parade—a curious custom that Will does not expect.

As the crowds withdraw to their tents, all drills cancelled for that afternoon, Will looks back to the grave where a handful of men go about the business of piling rock.

‡

That afternoon, Will meets Robert by the river. The dark blond waters slip past on their slow course to the ocean. Robert is washing something in the cut-banks, dark silt past his boots.

"Find something?" Will asks, and the question startles the other man. Sends him rocking forward toward the water. His one hand outstretched breaks the fall, but wets the sleeve of his tunic.

"Sorry," says Will, starting out over the silt. Picking his way carefully.

"I didn't suspect I was being watched," Robert smiles, head lowered. It is an awkward gesture for a man of his stature. He extends the object toward Will, who accepts it as soon as he is close enough to reach.

"A fossil," he says, surprised. It is a blue-coloured stone about the length of the first knuckle on his ring finger, a tooth perhaps.

"Odontolite," says Robert. "The presence of iron phosphate changes its colour. Some call it bone turquoise."

"It's beautiful," says Will, and means it.

"I've found others," he says, opening a small sack tied with a drawstring. The same sack he uses to collect soapstone.

Two tiny cochlea fall into the palm of his hand. "Snails," he says. "Ancient, of course."

Will takes the tiny artifacts into his own hands, pushes them around with the tip of his finger. "How do you know that they're ancient?"

"It's what we call a 'stone core' fossil," he answers. "When the animal dies and subsequently rots, it leaves an empty shell. This fills with sand over time, and eventually turns to stone. This takes a long time, of course."

"How did you know to look here?" asks Will.

"Not here," says Robert. "There."

Will follows the man's finger to a rock shelf thirty yards off.

"You need undisturbed sedimentary deposits. The kind you find in quarries, or where a river has exposed the rock face over time." He slides the spectacles up his nose.

"Robert, what are you doing here?" asks Will, looking up from the handful of fossils. "I mean, what are you doing *here*, in South Africa. The war?"

Robert gathers the tiny treasures back from Will, and pulls the drawstring tight. For a moment, he looks to the horizon, as though searching for an answer.

"I don't know," he says. "Sorry."

‡

Morale is low after the funeral. The camp is subdued. With no drills to occupy his time, Mason is agitated and impatient. Will can see it in his body movements before he reaches the man's tent.

"This is just wrong, Will," he says as the young man approaches him.

"What is?"

"This heat. One hundred and one degrees. Last night it was ninety-six with no sun."

Will can see that he has just returned from the trough pump. His hair is damp and tousled. The undershirt dark down the back.

Hardy arrives from the direction of the new depot. Large sweat stains expand like balloons beneath his arms.

"What's the news?" asks Mason.

"Not good," says Hardy, slightly pale. "Last night, only fifteen miles north at Enslin Siding, a thousand Boer raiders hit the supply train. It took two companies of Northhamptons, the Seaforth High-landers, and even the Lancers down from the Modder River to drive them off. They dynamited part of the track too."

"Casualties?"

Hardy nods.

Mason throws his towel down in the dust. Sets his hands against his hips.

"We're losing the goddamn war, boys."

‡

That evening Will visits the Kaffir hut, not so much for the food as the company. The balloonist's wife serves him a portion of dried meat and purple beer, much like his previous meal. The children run in and around the hut, chasing after one another in various states of undress. All of them are shoeless. The eldest boy wears linen trousers and a sleeveless shirt under a cloth vest. The younger ones wear coveralls, and the lone girl, a jumper. They are singing a children's rhyme that is somehow familiar to Will, but ultimately escapes him.

When Campbell arrives, he is dirtier than usual. A grease mark stretches from the corner of his eye to the edge of his mouth. He has been checking up on the balloon.

"Wait, I will join you," he says indicating the cup of yeasty beer. "I told you it was an acquired taste," he calls from inside the hut, and follows with a knowing laugh.

"What is it made from?" asks Will.

"Don't know, and don't want to know," he says tapping the visitor's mug with his own. Campbell downs half the liquid in one shot. "Ahhh."

"You're working on the balloon," says Will, indicating the grease.

"Yes. We're gathering hydrogen gas. It's a complicated procedure, involving sulphuric acid and iron. We run the gas we produce through a lime purifier. Won't be long now."

"Does it scare you?"

"What, flying?"

"No, the war."

"Bah. I'm above all that," Campbell says, and slaps his knee, laughing heartily. "It's those on the ground that need to be worried." The man's laughter ends too abruptly, as though he realizes too late what he has been saying.

It dawns on Will that Campbell has already partaken of the purple beverage today, and that he is not being honest about the war.

Will presses on, "What about your wife, your kids?"

"Hmph. Better off without me." Just then, one of the smaller boys crashes into his father's legs. "Oh," he exclaims, and lifts the child onto his hip.

"Do you know what *Kaffir* means?" he asks Will, but looks at his child. "It means 'infidel,'" Campbell adds, without waiting. "It's a derogatory expression. A name given to the natives by the Muslims, centuries ago. Funny thing, language."

Will thinks of all the times he used the term Kaffir since his arrival. "I didn't know," he says. The beer is already clouding his thoughts.

"Bantu is the correct term," Campbell says, putting the child down. "Xhosa, actually. Drink up. We'll have another." Campbell calls to his wife through the opening in the hut. "Lucky to have some left," he says, nodding at Will's cup. "Barrett discovered the delights of local brewing." The man winks. "Had to beat him off with a stick last night."

Will ignores Campbell's last comments, hoping to steer the conversation back to the subject of his wife. "How long have you been married?" he tries.

But the black woman arrives with two more cups, interrupting the inquiry. She is wearing the same short fringe apron and head scarf as always. Her hair is plaited underneath, and decorated with coral seeds, ivory, and bits of bone, which make it appear longer than it is. The plaits are gathered together in a beaded head ring. Her cheeks are freckled.

Campbell pats her on the ass as she returns to the hut. Just as quickly, she lands a backhanded swat behind his ear. Purple beer spills over his shirt, blending immediately with the growing mosaic of colours.

"Too long," says the balloonist, and Will realizes that it is the answer to his earlier question.

"Can I ask how?"

"This isn't about the birds and the bees, is it? Because ..."

Will flushes red, and Campbell laughs. Both men drink their beer. Will is almost enjoying it. The evening is actually comfortable. The sun low, lighting the big man. Forcing him to squint. But there is a breeze, easing the heat.

"When I came back from England," Campbell begins, suddenly serious, looking at a fixed point somewhere in the distance, "I bought a little farm. Nothing much. A few cattle. An orchard. A place to lay my head. I traded some with a Bantu village. It was an isolated place. The farm and the village. I'd have gone mad without the social contact. Anyway, the village head tells me one day that I need a wife. And he has a daughter, widowed a year earlier."

Campbell glances over his shoulder in the direction of the hut. Will wonders where the children have made off to.

"Well, the prospect of a woman sat okay with me," he continues. "So, like any other economic arrangement, we agreed on a *lobola*, a certain number of cattle."

Will's eyes expand.

"Mmm," says Campbell, sipping from his cup. "Got to rename her, too. My prerogative as a husband. So I chose Siphokazi—which means 'gift.' Though I just call her Sophie, for short. The truth is, her father took pity on me and sent her over to straighten out the farm. Isn't that right, Soph?" Campbell catches her approach by the rattling of seashells at her wrists.

"You drink too much," she says, in a perfect English baritone. "Ruins you in bed."

Campbell raises an eyebrow as she retreats with their spent cups. "Now that's a woman, lad."

‡

Will awakens to the sound of birds and thinks the world has ended. It is before dawn and the sky is still dark, just turning blue. He walks naked from his tent into the African veldt to watch them pass. Hordes of dark shapes shuttle overhead in a ruckus of wingbeats and noise. All of them headed south in a great migration. Fleeing, it seems, the calamity of war in the north. And underneath their harried cries and erratic flight, there is the sound of a distant thunder. A rolling chorus of cannon and guns.

Will stands alone in the wide expanse of plateau listening and watching as the sky lightens, and he is there still when the reveille is sounded. Early, he thinks, which can only mean one thing. It is odd that he did not miss them before. The birds. But he is sure, now that they are here in such tumultuous flight, that he has not heard them since his arrival in South Africa. Where do they go? he wonders. Where is their safe haven and how do they know when to return? Now that he knows what it's like to fly, Will feels a certain communion with their passage, arcing over the curved dome of the earth.

It is almost dawn before the last of the birds has passed, and Will is still standing naked on the veldt, the object of some attention now. Soldiers rubbing sleep from their eyes. Others lathering up for a quick shave at the enamel washbasins, propped between three sticks. The tents will be coming down this morning, Will thinks. No time to waste.

3

Belmont Garrison

December 10, 1899 –

February 12, 1900

a train of open trucks arrives at nine o'clock to ferry the troops north to Belmont Garrison. The men pile into the iron boxes as best they can. Some sit lined along the outer walls facing the soldiers across from them. Others lie prostrate down the middle of the floor and use their helmets to shield their eyes from the sun. Will sits on the outer edge of one of the cars with Robert and Mason on either side of him. The metal exterior is hot to the touch. He will be blistered by day's end.

Campbell rejoins the Royal Engineers in a slow-moving wagon train. Will does not think to see him again. When the train lets fly a blast from the steam whistle, a final goodbye to the Orange River camp, the balloonist waves his telltale handkerchief.

The twenty-five miles to Belmont takes almost three hours, but one of the black boys tells the men that this is good. Since the war began, the trip has taken as long as seven. The slow-moving leviathan snakes its way over culverts and sheer cliff faces, sand banks and veldt, on its way to the British garrison. Tunnels have been carved through the heart of two-hundred-foot kopjes.

When he arrives, Will is burned by the wind and choked by the billowing smoke, but the trip is worth it. The railway junction has a pleasant single-storey station house, plastered in white stucco with a pitch roof and two white chimneys. Behind the station and across the dusty road is a small hotel, similarly stuccoed with delicate iron balconies and shuttered windows of a European style. Farther along the track, at the end of the extended platform, there is a large goods shed and a variety shop, not unlike his uncle's.

The troops are billeted three miles from the station, according to a rumour running through the men. A short march, but that will mean lunch is delayed. In full gear at the height of the sun, Will feels as though he is melting. The profusion of sandflies adds to the aggravation as they set off down the limestone road in the direction of the converted farm, swatting indiscriminately. Robert, who is older and more portly than Will, appears on the verge of collapse as they near the long lane that leads to the camp. Mason, on the other hand, is spry and in high spirits.

The farm itself is a desert oasis of shade trees and grass. There is a large vegetable garden out back and a henhouse by the barn. The manor itself is very close in appearance to the train station, only there are flower boxes in the windows and a kitchen off the rear with a lean-to roof. A stone well powered by a windmill pump, however, is the immediate attraction of the parched soldiers.

Will strips to the waist by the stone cistern and, cupping his hands, pours the water over his head. The rivulets run the length of his exposed torso and are absorbed by the waist of his khaki trousers.

Already in the fields, several hundred yards east of the house, white troop tents are pitched—P Battery of the Royal Horse Artillery. Will and the others loaf in the shade of the first real trees they have seen in weeks. The officers meet on the open verandah. They will be discussing troop placement, but until they come to a decision about the Canadians, Will is content where he is. If he closes his eyes, he can almost forget that there is a war at all.

‡

Later, Mason convinces Will to accompany him into the surrounding kopjes. The bodies of dead Boer rebels remain uncovered as yet. The remnants of a skirmish the week before. The allies were given direct orders not to proceed, but to remain on the farm. However, several others have already been out and returned with hunting knives, pistols, and flop caps. Will agrees only to keep Mason out of trouble. He has little actual desire to see the dead Boer.

The surrounding slopes are steep and full of stinging nettles and thorns. Fortunately, it is early evening and the sun is not so intense. The officers were not exact in their depiction of the battle, and at first, the men find nothing but rocks—glacial rubble cast haphazardly over the hill amid weeds and twisted grass. However, the stench of rotting flesh is unmistakable.

It is Will who eventually comes across the first corpse. He does not signal Mason right away. Instead, he approaches the body for a closer inspection. It is a man of about fifty. Medium build. He has the characteristic square beard Will has heard attributed to the Boer, but he is surprised to find him dressed in a three-piece suit, complete with gold watch fob.

The watch would be considered quite a trophy among the other soldiers, but Will cannot bring himself to take it, even though he is certain the British troops will pillage the dead in the coming days. He removes the flop hat instead and scrambles up the slope in search of Mason.

His friend asks, "Did you come across any?"

"No," Will lies. "But I found this. You can have it."

Mason tries the cap on. It gives him a roguish look.

"Thanks," he says, examining it thoroughly. "Are you sure?"

"Yes," says Will. "Let's get back to camp before someone notices that we're gone."

Mason nods and slaps Will on the shoulder. Clearly, the gift pleases him. And the tension Will has felt mounting between them over the last few weeks thaws somewhat. Slowly, they pick their way down to the plateau floor.

‡

Mason received a small-calibre rifle for his thirteenth birthday, a tiny fowling piece. Will remembers his friend's excitement as the two of them waded into the prairie outside town, alone for the first time. Mason cradled the rifle like a child. Will carried a sack filled with drink bottles and soup cans. The orchestra of clanking and rattling scared off every animal for miles.

At a wood-beam fence line, Will emptied the contents onto the earth and then carefully placed the targets along the uppermost log. Mason fed cartridges into the breech as his father had demonstrated. It was a beautiful, clear blue day, without a hint of clouds. His friend squinted into the sun as he aimed the gun at the first mark in the line, a translucent green soda bottle. Will crouched in the high grass just behind Mason's shoulder, covering his ears.

The innocent crack of the firing pin was misleading. An instant later the bottle shattered. Mason turned to him and smiled, his eyes dancing with excitement. Will felt an almost religious sincerity as Mason passed the rifle to him.

He had never fired a gun before that moment. And Mason's voice buzzed in his ear as he whispered last-minute advice. But in the instant prior to pulling the trigger, Will heard nothing but the prairie wind. He stared down the line of the rifle at the brown syrup bottle, ten yards away, and squeezed the trigger. He did not even hear the sound of his own gun before the glass exploded. It was the slap of Mason's hand on his shoulder that shook him from the trance.

The two boys made their way through the targets in short order after that, resetting the tin cans several times each.

The walk back to town was quiet after the constant pop and smash of the shooting, and their shrill laughter afterward. Will dragged the empty sack behind him like a shadow. When Mason pulled up short, just before the dirt road leading into Portage, Will almost knocked him over, he was so lost in his thoughts. Not twenty paces off, on the edge of a piling, sat a fat black crow, preening itself in the late afternoon haze.

Without speaking, Mason dropped to one knee, while Will stood transfixed, an arm's length from his friend. With the same practised motions they had repeated all afternoon, Mason set the bird in his sights. Unlike their earlier targets, the crow did not shatter or explode with a satisfying dissonance. It did not even caw. The bird simply folded over and landed in the rushes.

The enormity of Mason's actions struck Will immediately, like an awful sinking in the pit of his stomach. But Mason was already off running, jumping through the grass.

"I got him," he yelled. "Did you see that, Will? Did you see that?"

‡

Belmont, because of its proximity to the rail station and the size of the force amassed there, has a higher concentration of blacks. Some are employed to offload supply trains. Others drive the army's wagons or perform any number of menial tasks. The army is a floating city toward which they migrate for opportunity.

Will has exchanged a few words with several young men who frequent Siphokazi's hut. But generally, fraternization with the blacks is frowned upon, and several men in the regiment have taken to openly ridiculing the labourers, who often do not understand the English taunts.

Will can chalk the behaviour up to simple racism, but he knows that it runs deeper than that. With each new Boer raiding success along British supply lines, the animosity toward the blacks grows. Many of the soldiers suspect them of spying, and the restlessness of months without a single full-on engagement—a chance at restitution—only heightens their frustration.

But none of this knowledge prepares Will for what he encounters outside a bell tent one evening after mess.

He is alone, not having seen Mason all day, when he comes across the small cluster of soldiers. Several wheel around to greet him, and immediately Will can tell that something is wrong.

He can hear sobbing coming from the open tent flap.

"Get lost," one of the soldiers says to him, tentatively, almost apologetically. His voice is rusted and grinds. The words catch.

The soldier next to him lets the tent flap fall closed. With greater conviction, he adds, "Move along, eh. Nothing to concern you." He crosses his arms over his chest. Will has seen him before. Knows the face.

A handful of onlookers peels away, leaving just the two men who spoke to Will. The men are from different companies, neither from his own. He wonders if they would greet Mason similarly.

Without thinking, Will approaches the tent. In spite of their rough greeting, the men part and allow him to pass. He looks into both sets of eyes separately and deliberately, searching for some sign of what he might expect, but both men look away.

When Will parts the flap, a shock of dying light penetrates the gloom. This wedge falls across a black boy on his knees. His arms are bound behind his back, but what jumps out immediately is the mess of the boy's face. Swollen and glistening with a purple smear of his own blood, the head is ruined. One eye has disappeared completely in a tumour of raw flesh.

Will opens his mouth, but nothing comes out. It is then he realizes that the boy has no pants. The hairless sex bobs innocently between his legs, just below the dun-coloured tails of his soiled shirt.

The child's face lolls upwards to gaze upon him.

One of the soldiers inside the tent spits on the ground, awakening Will from his momentary trance. The man is partially undressed, wearing only his shirtsleeves.

"What are you doing?" asks Will, as though perhaps a logical explanation can be proffered.

"Fuck off."

The threat of violence is suddenly close to him, like the metallic stench of the boy's blood, and something else. What is it? he thinks. His mind scrambles. And then he sees the second soldier on the far side of the tent, facing away, methodically buttoning his trousers, hoisting his suspenders.

Before Will can react, he is grabbed from behind by the two men he passed on the way in. Too late, he pulls away, struggling to free himself. Wanting to lash out blindly, to hurt.

The man in his shirtsleeves punches him in the stomach, driving the wind from his chest.

In his ear, one of the others says, "We caught him stealing. The ungrateful bastards. After what we've done for them."

And in spite of his predicament, Will wants to laugh at the absurdity of this assertion. But he can't even draw breath.

Outside the tent again, the soldiers toss him to the ground. Cramped, Will rolls onto all fours, battling his way through the pain, attempting to re-enter the tent. But a boot overturns him easily, and he stares dumbly up at the soldier who punched him. The man's face is blood-spattered. Beads of it in his moustache. He is casually buttoning his shirt.

"I don't know what Mason sees in you," he says.

The other soldiers do not look as convinced. Behind his aggressor, the black boy escapes into the evening, hobbling, and rocking, and clutching his clothes to his chest.

‡

In the days that follow, Will tries more than once to broach the topic with Mason. The brief friendship between him and Robert completely breaks down. He wallows in his own shame.

Twice he approaches Captain Blanchard, but in the end he does nothing. Tells no one. He is shocked by his own impotence.

After a week, the routine of Belmont covers his wound like a scab. And then he sees the boy at the railway siding, bruised still, but healing. Will attempts to speak with the boy, but he does not seem to know him. Can it be? Will wonders.

Up close, the boy's right eye is still sealed, the colour of aubergine and curdled milk. Infected.

Will tries to convince the lad to accompany him to the authorities. Make a report. But the boy only stares at him through his one good eye as though he were mad. He does not speak enough English, and after several minutes of unsuccessful hand gestures, the discussion breaks down completely.

The boy must get back to work. He tries to apologize to Will in broken English, and then disappears down the siding.

‡

Following the afternoon's exercises on Scots Kopje, Will and Mason queue up outside the mess tent to receive the evening meal. Rumour suggests fish. The scent upon the air suggests a military version of stew. Will is exhausted. Physically, he is sick of the desert. His face is burnt a shade of roast turkey. His uniform is filthy. Mason doesn't look much better. But the added weight of the rape has settled permanently across Will's shoulders, like a yoke. He can't shake the memory of the tent. He remembers its salty-iron reek on his tongue.

For reasons that are yet unclear to him, Will is unable to relate the incident to Mason. He could lie to himself and say that they have grown apart lately—that the war has somehow come between them—and perhaps this lie would not be so far from the truth after all. However, Will knows that he would never have shared this sort of story with Mason. Not even at the best of times. Boundaries and borders have always underwritten their friendship.

Only now these borders have been fortified with something more. Will is too ashamed to lay his impotence before Mason. At each turn since his arrival in South Africa, Will has been tested and found wanting.

As the two men draw alongside the cookstove, a kitchen hand slops gruel into their tin bowls. The ooze of it sounds like a boot pulled from a pocket of mud.

"I think there's fish in here somewhere," smirks Mason, prodding the dish with his spoon.

Will turns away from the line, and is immediately bumped. Hard. His meal topples over the ground in a smear of grey and worm-coloured flesh. For a moment, the thought surfaces that perhaps in his fatigue he has been careless. He should have looked before peeling away from the mess tent. But this theory is only self-defence against what he knows just occurred.

The interloper dropped his shoulder into Will's, driving him backward several paces. He recognizes the back of the shaved head.

A second later the soldier spins, glances down at his soiled boots.

"Look what you've done!" he exclaims, too loudly for added effect. "You've gone and messed my boot." He is red in the face. Will imagines a walrus behind the bushy whiskers of the man's moustache.

There are two other men with him. Will recognizes only one—a guard from outside the tent.

Before Will can even consider a response, Mason tosses his own meal to the earth and shoves the larger man. "Piss off."

They grapple at each other's lapels. Walrus snatches a fist full of Mason's hair. A crowd leaps into place, surrounding them. And then Will is pummelled, tackled to the dust by one of his aggressor's chums.

The fight does not last more than a minute before a nearby sergeant orders several onlookers to break them apart. In the scuffle, Will has his eye gouged. The heat of a scratch burns beneath it on his cheek.

Standing, but still struggling for release, is Mason. His lip has been bloodied. The walrus simply dusts his shirt and smiles.

"That's enough, private!" The fat finger of the sergeant pokes at Mason's chest. "Clear off, the lot of ya."

Reluctantly, soldiers re-queue or take their meals elsewhere, away from the action.

"Against my better judgement," begins the sergeant, once the men are calm and the situation under his control, "I'm going to forget what I witnessed here today. But God help the next one of ya I have to discipline." He looks directly at Will and Mason as he says this. A dribble of tobacco juice sits in the corner of his lips.

"And you, Kadinsky," he continues, turning toward the walrus, "I've had just about enough of you. Let's see if we can't find ourselves a few latrines that need emptying."

The threat does not wipe away the soldier's smile. Even his companions try in vain to hide grins.

"Go on," the sergeant bellows. "Don't just stand there with your teeth in your mouth. Let's get you dandies some shovels."

Kadinsky blows Mason a kiss before leaving. At Will, he only stares, and then lays a finger over his lips, as though shushing a child.

Mason tucks in his shirt. "Good thing for him that sergeant came along." He too begins to grin uncontrollably, wiping the trickle of blood on his chin. "You know that guy?"

Will looks at the back of the shaved head in the distance.

"Hardy says he spent time in the Kingston Penitentiary."

Will lowers his head. "No," he answers. "I've never seen him before."

‡

The arrival of the first ambulance train shatters the oasis of calm at Belmont. The barn is converted into a field hospital and cots are shipped up from the south. The trains arrive from the front in Magersfontein where the Boer are still giving the British a hard time. Reports funnelled through Hardy say that the Dutch have dug in and now have miles of impregnable trench networks.

Will volunteers to help transfer patients from the station to the farm, but his real motives are twofold. The work is a way of forgetting, for one. And he does not want to miss the incoming trains, for another. The scores of wounded are accompanied by doctors and nurses from the advance field hospital, and he is hoping to meet Claire on one of the cars.

The stench of the ambulance trains is horrific, however, and too quickly Will realizes that the job of stretcher bearer is not an easy one.

Men come away from the front with wounds in every possible location. Legs and thighs are popular. There are numerous abdomen wounds as well. These are the victims of the Pom Pom guns. The soldiers report that the machine gun can cover an acre with bullets in under a minute, hitting many targets, killing and wounding soldiers. Others come in with shrapnel wounds in the face, throat, and lungs. More still have dysentery or fever. Will uses a converted two-wheeled cart known as a Boer ambulance to transport the wounded from station to farm, six miles round trip. After three separate voyages, he breaks for a supper of bread and hardtack. He has not seen Claire or her friend Hilde on the first two trains.

Just before dark, word of a third train arrives. Mason offers to take his place, but Will insists on making the journey. He jogs and quick steps the three miles to the station and arrives before the train. The muscles in his legs spasm. His mind is exhausted. The station master and his black boys light lamps along the platform in anticipation.

When the train pulls in, it is almost empty, but for a few walking wounded. Will is requested to ferry supplies, and to direct the transferred nursing staff. He recognizes Claire immediately as she steps off the train. The freckles. Strawberry hair. Rogue curls at her temples.

Will calls out to her, and when her eyes finally find his above the small crowd, she appears puzzled at first.

"Will Regan," he says, letting the cart alone. "We met in Cape Town," he continues, but already his heart is falling.

"Yes," she says. "Yes, we saw that awful play together." And then she smiles.

‡

The limestone road is eerily phosphorescent as the odd little parade marches on toward the farm. The wounded lean on one another for support, or make use of provisional crutches. Claire is one of only three nurses who arrived on the train. There is also a surgeon. Hilde will be among those to arrive in the morning. Conversation between Will and Claire is awkward and halting at first, but it is a long walk and they eventually find their pace—a meandering tempo, punctuated by occasional silences. They are both tired. The atmosphere, the circumstance, and the odds of having found each other make the trip back almost surreal for Will.

He asks, "Have you seen much action?"

"This is the closest we've come to the front," she answers, and the two walk on, Will wheeling the Boer ambulance full of medical supplies, Claire swinging her bag in step.

"You?" she says finally, picking the conversation up like a lost thread.

"This is it."

"You're lucky then."

"Don't say that to Mason."

"Who?"

Will breathes out all the tension he has been harbouring for weeks. A cool breeze greets them at the gate.

‡

Everyone is kept busy during the first weeks at Belmont, but no one so much as the nursing staff. Trains from Magersfontein continue to arrive daily. An almost constant thunder rolls in the north. Patients move in and out of the impromptu ward. The fortunate board trains to the south and eventually home. Others are patched up and returned to their regiments at the front. But many more are buried behind the farmhouse.

A few days later, trains begin to arrive from the south as well, bringing reinforcements, so that the farm at Belmont begins to truly resemble a garrison. The Queensland Mounted Infantry, the Royal Mounted Fusiliers, the Imperial Mounted Infantry, and the Munster Fusiliers all pitch their tents. Eventually the Canadians are reunited with the 2nd Duke of Cornwalls and the Shropshire Light Infantry as well.

Will continues his ambulance duties when he can in the afternoons, because it brings him into contact with Claire, but the regiment has fallen back into step with its Orange River routine. Will and the rest of the Winnipeg Rifles march out to Scots' Kopje every second morning after breakfast to practise the attack. And in the evenings, when the temperature drops, they march out into the desert to maintain their physical conditioning.

At other times the men are assigned random duties such as trench digging or grounds work. Will has also pulled pickets guarding the new ammo depot in the large-goods building, or shifted rail cars at the station. For the first time since their arrival in South Africa, both he and Mason are even sent out on night patrol in the kopjes, though neither finds reason to sound the alarm.

That whole first week, after Magersfontein, Will is charged with an energy he lacked previously. He feels useful, and the constant work is cathartic, after recent events. But mostly, his renewed energy comes from his proximity to Claire.

‡

The calamity of Magersfontein slowly trickles down to the troops at Belmont. Will and Mason are eating lunch in the mouth of their tent when Hardy arrives. Robert is napping behind them, but raises himself on one arm as the burly corporal begins to speak. Hardy runs a fat hand through his thinning sandy-blond hair and replaces his cap.

"The Highlanders bore the brunt of it," he says, still somewhat short of breath from the walk. "The Black Watch, the Seaforths. They were advancing at night in order to surprise the Boer. The Argylls and the Sutherlands were in the rear." Barrett, in a moment of rare sobriety, has written a story for the papers back home, says Hardy. The details are his.

"It was raining," he tells them. Only lightly at the time of their approach, but it had been pouring earlier. The men had previously been huddled two to a blanket in makeshift tents, awaiting the attack.

"Once the advance was underway, the greatest difficulty was maintaining formation. No moon. They couldn't see the man in front of them. So they had these scouts with a rope, stretched out on either end of the advance, penning in the front line."

The men made an effort to remain silent, but the rocky approach forced more than one to trip up, catch the boot of the soldier in front of him. They were ordered to hold the shoulder of the soldier next to them, so as not to spread the line too thin. And so the men in the regiment plodded forward almost as though they were part of a giant rugby scrum.

"The Boer were huddled in their trenches, waiting for them," Hardy says with a sneer, as though somehow he detected foul play.

Robert is sitting, his head visible through the tent awning.

"Go on," Mason huffs. No one is eating now.

"They'd set a wire up," he says. "The Boer, I mean. With tin cans attached to it."

The picture is becoming clear to Will. A thousand men creeping shoulder to shoulder toward an unseen enemy entrenched and guarded.

"They gave the order to fan out," says Hardy, "but it was too late."

The torrent of Mauser fire came all at once. The stream of lead cut the forward line to pieces. A few men from the Black Watch rushed forward and were slaughtered within feet of the Boer trench. Most turned to run, trampling the dead and the wounded. Others dug in, using their rifles, their helmets, their bayonets, and their hands. Fingernails were black and ruined with the effort.

"The lot of them were pinned throughout the night and through the next day. Artillery got a Maxim gun in line, but it was hopeless. The Boer guns shredded a cavalry attack attempting to bring relief."

It wasn't until nightfall of the second day that survivors were able to crawl back. Some dragged their dead and wounded comrades. When the official count was complete, the British had lost more than a thousand men.

"A private from the Seaforths tells me seven hundred were killed in the first five minutes."

Will realizes that he has not chewed his last mouthful throughout the entire story.

"It could have been us," he says. He remembers Mason's disappointment when the Gordons were called up, leaving the Royal Canadians to languish in the rear.

‡

From the opening in the hayloft, Claire can see the kopjes beyond the farm. She has begun to smoke a brand of Turkish cigarettes— El Kalif—blowing white clouds out over the yard. A surgeon turned her on to them. Said it calmed the nerves. Her feet are tired, yet she dare not sit or remove her shoes for fear that she will not be able to continue afterward. Instead she leans against the rough grain of the wooden transom. She has learned to sleep while standing.

Belmont is a pleasant place. Were it not for the groves of white tents in the fields, she might even call it beautiful. Perhaps it is the trees. The wounded lounge beneath them on the front lawn, sharing stories with the eager reinforcements. None so eager, she thinks, as the Canadians. Mason was eager the moment he stepped off his ship in Cape Town. She thought him silly then, and perhaps a bit naive. He has not come to visit her yet, though surely Will has mentioned her arrival. She saw him fetching water from the stone well early this morning after the rouse had sounded, dressed only in his trousers, his newly brown body a target for the sun. She cannot imagine him shaving, though. The square jaw-line smooth as polished alabaster.

Below her, on the ward, it is she that does the shaving. So many men. But there is one she need not touch. Most of his face is missing now. A miracle of life, says Sister Martha. But Claire thinks only aberration. His speech is a mottled gurgle she cannot understand, though she suspects he's after water. They all are. The ward is in constant thirst. But she is better here, at the hospital. Even Hilde agrees that anything is better than the advanced dressing station. A tent—a gazebo, really—with open sides. Sand festering in every wound. And the noise. The awful moaning and the pitiful cries. Mouths opening, twisting in agony, quieted only by the more impressive guns. Then the tent is full of mimes.

The other soldier, Will, was back again this afternoon, transporting the wounded. Hilde calls him The Bump, as in bump on a log. But Claire likes him, his quiet self-possession. His shyness is so different from Mason's aggression, or the rude talk of the Tommies. The doctor downstairs does not pass her by without a pat on the arse. She suspects Will to have a crush on her, but the soldier is even younger than his friend. How could she? she thinks, and butts the dying embers against the wall.

She came to South Africa to escape her parents' relentless hunt for a husband for her. Or, at least, that was part of the reason. Were it not for the small stipend her nana left her, she would still be in Albury, pining. She and Hilde and another woman from the Melbourne Nurses College anted up to be here. The first official Australian nursing contingent had not even been considered when she embarked, at her own expense, with the troops.

Of course the war was nothing more than an idea to her then. A way out. The last two weeks have been an awakening—a slow, grudging admission of her father's wisdom. Her initiation at the field hospital in Magersfontein hit her like the concussion of an exploding shell. She felt as though all oxygen had been siphoned from the medical tent the moment the first stretcher bearers arrived, slinging shattered bodies between them.

Sister Martha slapped her into action, and afterwards, Claire was shocked at her capacity to function, operate on instinct. In fact, the relentless triage kept her sane in the early hours. She didn't have a chance to cry until Belmont.

‡

On Friday, the ambulance train arrives while Will is storming an invisible enemy on Scots' Kopje. The Canadians, as they have since De Aar, take the hill and march promptly back to camp. The quartermaster opens his larder for lunch, and the troops are treated to a forkful of fish just in from the coast. Satisfied, Will strolls over to the ward to see Claire.

The day before he purchased a pat of chocolate at the shop behind the station while he was waiting for the train from Magersfontein. Although it was dear, he decided to buy it anyway. He told himself that it would do well to keep his spirits up during the forthcoming sorties being discussed by the British Colonel Pilcher, but his plan all along was to pass it on to Claire.

He is fortunate to find her on the lawn sharing a cigarette with Hilde beneath the big trees. The other nurse leaves at the sight of Will's approach, and he is glad not to have to face her again. Claire's body leans like a length of willow branch against the ancient trunk, and he can see that she is exhausted. The rumbling in the north has quieted in the last two days, and the trains carry only fever patients now, but the ward is full.

As Will steps within earshot, she asks, "All played out?" He has explained the morning war games to her already.

"I brought you something," Will answers, unfolding the foil he keeps in his pocket.

Claire drops the cigarette. "You're such a darling," she exclaims. "Shall I eat it now?"

"Before it melts," says Will.

Claire rolls her eyes and tosses her head in mock ecstasy as she tastes the first bite. She smiles then at her own pantomime and shrugs her shoulders in a laugh.

"Would you like any?"

"No, thanks."

"Good."

Will smiles in return. "It looks like we're to finally see some action," he tells her as she eats. But the girl's eyes change then, and she swallows the mouthful prematurely.

Licking her lips, she says, "Not to the front?"

Will is surprised by Claire's reaction. "No," he says. "Not just yet. A sortie. Or at least that's the buzz. Might not happen till after Christmas," he reassures her.

Claire sinks to the earth with her back propped against the tree and sighs. "You'll help me if I can't get back up, won't you? I haven't sat down for days, it seems. Not till lights out anyway. And even then, there's always someone crying out."

Will sits cross-legged facing her. She has a pout like a child, exaggerated almost, letting off steam. He wants to kiss her then.

"Bloody war," she says and takes another bite of the candy. Claire smiles at the petulance of her own behaviour, and gives him a wink. "You'll spoil me."

A silence falls over the two as an unexpected breeze rustles in the leaves. Men from every regiment walk past. A periodic clink from a nearby game of horseshoes reaches them, and laughter bubbles over from the verandah where several officers hold court.

"Thanks," Claire says. "For the chocolate."

‡

Will watches a group of Canadian soldiers plan their attack. The ostrich ignores them. It stands at least two heads above the tallest of the men, blinking into the sun—part of a small flock that arrived during the night. The cock is a beautiful animal with black metallic plumage over its back, and long white tufts of down at the tips of its wings.

The soldiers break into a loose circle around the bird, shuffling sideways like monkeys, their arms dangling. The ostrich cranes its long pink neck and swallows, taking note of the invaders for the first time. More curious than afraid. It bats a pair of thick black lashes, takes a step on powerful two-toed feet.

"Now," yells one of the men, and the soldiers converge on his order.

Incongruously, the bird roars like a lion, stopping the closest of the men in his tracks. One of the privates slips to his ass in the red earth. The feline growl terminates in a protracted hiss.

Undeterred, a third soldier lunges from the rear, making a grab for the exposed nape. The bird spins in response, throwing the would-be rider, who rolls in a cloud of dust. The next man over receives a hooked toe in the centre of his chest, tossing him backward like a rag doll.

And then, through the opening of his own creation, the ostrich runs. An incredible acceleration that leaves the men stunned.

Soldiers gathered by Will are in tears with laughter. The hapless attackers help their comrades to their feet. The failed rider takes a bow.

As the men break up and head off in different directions, Will lingers, looking out over the veldt, unable to share their joviality. It has been days since he's seen the black boy at the siding, and today he began to ask around. Most of the other boys simply ignored him, or feigned ignorance over the language barrier. But finally, he cornered a younger boy in the storeroom.

"I just want to help," he said, yelling almost, in desperation.

And scared more by the tone of Will's language, the boy opened up.

From what Will could gather, the infection had spread and now the child was feverish, bedridden. Will has kept the secret from Mason for too long, and now he feels that it is impossible to ask him for help.

The only other person he can think of is Claire. But even that involves complicated explanations. Admissions on his part that shame him.

He has managed to steer clear of Kadinsky since the incident outside the mess, but constantly he lives in fear of encountering the man again. His fear is not a fear of the physical harm Kadinsky could no doubt inflict, but a fear of the further humiliations he might suffer as a result of the man's actions. In fact, just knowing that Kadinsky is aware of Will's cowardice is enough to instil in him a campaign of avoidance.

Will sighs. Claire is his only hope.

‡

Claire waits for him at the windmill. She has risen early to wash and dress. Her long red hair is down and combed for the first time since she left Sydney. She is careful to avoid Sister Martha's accusatory glare on her way through the ward, and now she feels foolish. Soldiers from the various troops nod and smile as they dip their buckets in the cistern. She can only envision what they think of her. But finally he arrives, strutting like a small god, tanned and smooth, his hair grown back from its early shearing, so that now a lock dips over his brow. He smiles like a villain.

"Hello," he greets her. "Will told me you were here." Mason reaches into the water with both hands and splashes his face. He shakes his head like a dog afterward.

She imagines him a young Heathcliff, and herself as Catherine. The sky is clear, as it has been for more than a week. The sun is just rising behind him.

"You haven't visited," she says cheerfully, but hates the sound of her voice. "I had begun to think you'd forgotten me."

"Who could forget a face like that?" he says and beams at his blatant flattery.

"Your friend tells me you might be leaving on an expedition."

"Boer raiders," he says, filling his bucket. "Somewhere between here and Douglas. Maybe we'll catch them unaware." Mason turns to leave, and then stops. Over his shoulder he says, "Hey, maybe we could go for a walk sometime."

"Maybe," she answers.

Mason smiles.

‡

Will catches her as she is leaving the ward in the barn. Her uniform is marked with russet stains. Her hair dishevelled. She looks weary. Wearier, perhaps, when she realizes it is Will who is hailing her, though he hopes this last observation is imagined.

"Have I caught you at a bad time?" he asks as he draws nearer, wondering if ever there is a good time during a war.

"No, sorry. I was expecting someone else." She smiles a lopsided grin. "It's been a long day."

"Yeah." Will looks at the ground.

"What is it?"

"I don't want you to think ill of me." Clouds scuttle along the horizon above her head. In the distance a train whistle bellows like a lost calf.

"What?"

Claire's head tilts to one side, and Will thinks again, as he has many times before, that she is beautiful.

"I need your help."

Will tries only to be factual, but he also wants to be thorough in his explanation. The story, when spoken aloud, is raw. It does not fit around his tongue. His throat constricts with its telling. And slowly, as his narrative of violence unfolds, Will watches Claire's beautiful face twist into a mask of disgust and horror.

Her silence, however, is the worst part. Will is relieved when finally she breaks it with a question.

"And you know them? The men who did this?"

Will nods, but cannot look her in the eye. The indictment is only thinly veiled beneath her words. "Some of them. One in particular."

"And where is the boy now?"

Will explains where he thinks the village is. "We'd have to walk. And we could get in a lot of trouble."

"Nonsense." Claire turns and walks quickly back toward the barn. "I'll need a few things," she yells over her shoulder. "We'll leave immediately."

‡

Claire tells Sister Martha that she will not be back this afternoon. "Woman's problem," she whispers.

And the old nun nods, although she is in no way pleased nor in accord.

Claire takes everything she will need out of the ward in her skirts, and she has Will place them in his haversack. Her hands shake, and her anger, unassigned to any one target, is difficult to conceal.

She can sense Will's guilt like a set of irons he drags behind him. His need for absolution is perceptible. But she cannot give it to him yet. Part of her wishes to throttle him for his misplaced sense of persecution, instead.

They decide together that the best subterfuge is not to hide at all, and so they set out across the veldt following a cattle trail to the closest kopjes. It is the same route that the African labourers follow each day arriving and departing. The dusty track is only wide enough for a single-file march, and Claire spends much of the trip staring at Will's back—the sad slope of his shoulders, the raw burn across his neck.

They hope that their blatant departure from Belmont will lead anyone who sees them to assume they have been granted the necessary permissions. And in the end, it works.

They do not speak much in the beginning. Whether it is their anxiety over getting caught, or Will's shame in divulging the events that have led them here, Claire cannot tell. But it gives her much time to sort through the conflicting emotions she has experienced since Will divulged his secret to her.

"I'm glad you came to me," she tells him finally, once they are out of view of the Belmont Garrison.

Will does not respond, at first. But after several strides, he stops and looks back over his shoulder. The smile is weak, but it is there.

As they pick their way around loose boulders into the hills, the track widens into an expanse of crushed stone and scree. The day is hot, as is every day at Belmont, but there is some breeze to relieve the flies. And in the end, if Claire tries, she can imagine that they are out for a stroll in the fields beyond her childhood home in Australia.

Once they crest the slope of the kopje, the village, which has moved closer to the garrison so that the boys can access the army's paying jobs, comes into view. The cattle are gathered in a kraal at the centre of a group of more than twenty wattled huts. Smoke rises from the evening's cook fires. Activity is slow and lackadaisical.

An older gentleman greets them at the edge of the circled huts. He is small and bent and uses a stick to support himself. His tufts of white curly hair have grown erratic. When he speaks, Claire can see only one tooth.

Through mime and gesture she is able to make the man

understand that she is here to help the boy, and after a prolonged nodding of his head, he leads them slowly to a hut on the far side of the kraal.

A scrawny dog, no more than a rib cage and tail, follows them, sniffing and barking intermittently. Several of the younger children shadow them from a distance. Some naked, with only a bone necklace. The eldest in simple frocks, or knickers.

Women, as though drawn intuitively to the spectacle, step from their homes to observe their approach.

"The men have all gone off to work the supply trains and wagon columns," Will says in a soft voice.

At the entrance to the hut, a woman, who Claire guesses is the boy's mother, stops them and shouts something at Will.

The old man tries to calm her, but she continues to shout, pushing past him until she is only inches from Will's chest, pointing and gesticulating. Claire watches as Will accepts the woman's admonishments on behalf of the monsters who hurt her son. The woman strikes him once with a closed fist against his chest, as though she were pounding on a door that would not let her in.

Finally, however, she is spent and crying. The elderly man leads her back to the hut. Claire follows through the cloth curtain, leaving Will outside.

Beyond the doorway, the scent of infection is rampant. Claire holds a cloth to her nose as she approaches the boy, who lies next to the wall on a woven mat. His face is swollen up like a full water bladder. His features stretched and flattened.

The mother is collapsed beside him, stroking his limp hand.

"What is his name?" she asks the distraught mother. "My name is Claire."

"Uuka," the woman sobs. "Uuka."

Claire hears the curtain brushed aside, and knows that Will is watching her.

"Can you help him?"

Claire sighs. "He has a tremendous fever. I'll have to drain the pus from the wound and show the mother how to change the dressings after we're gone. But the fever is the real danger."

The case is not an impossible one, Claire knows. She has been patching up men for weeks now. Many worse than this. She is good at her job, and she takes great pride in it. Lately, however, she has begun to question the efficacy of healing the physical body. What she would really like is the ability to delve deeper, to explore the psychic wounds she cannot see, cannot ever hope to heal, and with a sharpened knife, carve them out like tumours.

After a moment, she turns to take the haversack from Will, and sets to work.

‡

Will is quiet on the way back to Belmont. Claire administered a syringe to the boy and cleaned his wound carefully, so that by the time they left the fever had already begun to recede. She seems hopeful, and therefore, so is Will. But he is not happy.

The light in the sky is already fading. The sun will set soon and they will have to walk quickly if they are to make it back to Belmont before dark.

"Thank you," he says after several minutes of walking.

"Don't thank me yet. He's not out of the woods."

"I know," says Will. "I'm thanking you for trying."

Will cannot tell if she is blushing or flushed from the heat.

"Yes, well."

The shadows on the kopje are long as they begin their ascent. Along the way, they cross small pockets of Xhosa returning from the day's work. Each time they do, they raise their hands in salute, and the workers nod, move off the path, and allow them to pass.

"You know, not to say that the right thing has been done here," Claire says once Belmont is again on the horizon. "But I don't think much would have been different if you had reported the incident with Uuka."

Will studies Claire's face as they walk.

"Some lives are just more important than others out here. Uuka's just another casualty. I mean, what would they really do to these soldiers for harming an African?"

Will can see that Claire is trying hard not to cry. The afternoon's events are catching her up. He places a hand on her shoulder.

A moment later, Claire speaks. "I don't know what I imagined before I arrived here, but this isn't it."

The two of them pass the pickets with enough light left so as not to arouse alarm. The soldiers from the Shropshires say nothing as they walk past them into camp. For this, Will is relieved.

However, on the way to the nurse's tent, Kadinsky steps in front of them. Will sees him at the last moment, chatting with a nurse, and pulls up short.

Claire looks from Will to Kadinsky, whom she does not recognize. Will does not know what he expects to happen, but even the small group of soldiers and nurses hanging about can sense the tension. Their quiet talk comes to a halt in anticipation of they know not what.

"Found someone to tend to your nigger, then?"

Will's jaw flexes in response.

Claire's lips part as she begins to piece things together. "Is this him?" she says rather more loudly than necessary, an almost hysterical assertion more than an actual question. "Is it?"

But without waiting for a response Claire steps forward like Uuka's mother earlier, so that the top of her nurse's cap is level with Kadinsky's jutting chin.

It is clear from the nervous look on the man's face that he had not anticipated a challenge from Claire.

"Fancy yourself a soldier?" she asks.

"Aren't you a feisty one," says Kadinsky by way of response, glancing around at the crowd. But his forced humour does not ring true. Several of the nurses twitter with nervous laughter.

The man is still smiling at his own joke, however, when Claire slaps him across the face. Once with each hand. It happens so fast, Kadinsky does not even raise a hand in his own defence. And to Will's surprise, Claire stands her ground to watch his anger build uselessly, daring him to react. When she is sure the man will do nothing, she strides past him and through the flaps of her waiting tent.

A few other nurses exchange glances and follow, drawn by curiosity more than anything else. But some remain to watch the drama play itself out.

For a moment, Will is unsure what the man will do next. He braces himself in the event of an assault. But Kadinsky only wipes his lips with the back of his right hand, examining the trickle of blood left there, before walking away to the sound of the crowd and their hushed suppositions.

‡

The military train arrives directly out of a Jules Verne novel, hissing steam through obscene nostrils. Its hide is scarred with the bulbous scoring of an arc light, welded seams of iron connecting plates of metal two inches thick.

Everyone on the platform stops, including Will and Mason. Small eyes crowd the slit openings cut uniformly from the iron plates.

"Water," comes a disembodied voice from inside the belly of the beast.

"Yeah," yells another. "Give us a cup."

And fingers push through the holes, more calls for relief.

"Boer prisoners?" says Mason, looking in Will's direction.

"No. I think they're British soldiers."

"Please, lads."

Will detaches his water bottle and Mason does the same. Several other soldiers step off the platform and approach the iron giant.

"It must be a furnace in there," says Mason as someone grabs his bottle. He watches, incredulous, as it disappears.

"Let's see the Boer tackle that," says a British officer from the mouth of the station house.

"Piece of work," whistles another from the shaded interior.

Will reaches up to retrieve his empty bottle. More soldiers arrive with refills.

"This is how we'll win the war," says the British captain. "English innovation."

His colleague answers from within, "Seems a bit of a steamer for the men, though."

"Ah, well. Life isn't all beer and skittles, now is it?"

It has been almost a week since Will has spoken privately to Claire. Drills have been stepped up in light of the coming sortie, and an outbreak of enteric fever has the nurses busy again. But Will thinks of her always.

He has been coming down to the siding almost every day to look for Uuka as well, but to no avail.

But when he turns away from the monstrous train, he notices that a group of boys has gathered at the end of the platform to gawk at the technological wonder. And there in their midst, is Uuka. His face is still bandaged, but he is standing and jostling with the others. His body is rail thin. His face, dark and clouded. But he is there.

The captain shouts, "Hey, you lads! Get back to work. The army isn't paying for you to stand around, is it?"

At his command, the kids scatter. Uuka goes with them.

‡

Will and Mason gather with the other men outside the quartermaster's larder as he receives the shipment of Christmas goods. The big man bellows for breathing room over the craning, pushing crowd. All week, the rumours have been flying about the feast being provided out of Cape Town. The black boys from the station help offload the mule-driven wagon. Hundreds of pounds of turkey, goose, and duck have been promised by the officers. Plum pudding and dumplings. A ration of beer for every man.

But when the troops offer to help with the return trip, the Kaffirs shrug. There is no return trip. That's everything. Nine disconsolate hens. Two ducks and a starving turkey. Will breaks up a fight between a private from the Shropshires and one of the cook's assistants. A rather sallow-looking Mason stomps off in the direction of his tent.

Barrett's voice, as distinct as any sound, rises behind Will. "This simply will not do. No Christmas pudding? Bloody hell, man."

The quartermaster folds his sizeable arms across a barrel chest, but does not respond. For a moment, Will thinks the poor writer is about to cry. But instead, he raises an indignant hand. "The world shall know of this," he says without any sense of irony.

"I've no doubt," says the quartermaster.

Barrett strolls past Will in a huff without recognizing him. "And nary a drop, I'll bet," he mumbles.

It has been two months since the men left Quebec City aboard the *Sardinian*. Longer still since they left their homes. They have trekked through the sandstorms of De Aar, bivouacked in the swamps of Orange River, and stormed the imaginary Boer of Scots' and Enlsin Kopjes time and again, all the while surviving on bread without butter, hardtack, and the occasional serving of canned meat. Yet in all that time, they have not fired a single shot in defence of the South African colony.

It is a difficult Christmas, thinks Will, as the men continue to push and elbow around him. And not just for Barrett.

‡

Christmas just isn't Christmas without snow. Will remembers one holiday in particular when he awakened long before his uncle John or his aunt Mary. She was still alive then. The night before the streets had been aglow beneath a sheen of ice. The product of a late-season rain. The fields around Portage were turned and frozen in clumps of dark angry earth, broken stalks of hay and wheat.

But the snow had come throughout the night in slow fat flakes, and eventually in a wet torrent just before dawn as the temperature continued to rise. Will bundled himself in scarf and hat and mittens—entered the blue half-light of the snow, kicking at drifts.

He gathered his first snowball of the season, and packing it to perfection, he refused to throw it—to let the moment end. Instead, he placed it in the powder at his feet and proceeded to roll it into the bottom third of a snowman. When he was through, the ball was nearly half his height. Stacking the next two spheres became a challenge, and yet, when he was finished, the world behind his uncle's store was inhabited by a giant.

The snowman lasted throughout Christmas in spite of the afternoon snowball fights and games of capture the flag which raged around it. He saw the New Year come and go.

He did not disappear completely until the warm winds of March arrived, wasting him slowly to a puddle of his former self.

Though the onset of spring brought its own sense of excitement and beginning, Will watched the snowman with a pang of sadness at the end of each new day. He wished he could have captured its perfection in a photograph and carried it with him always.

‡

Mason is admitted to the ward for stomach pains and a rising temperature. It is two days after Christmas and Will and Hardy both sit on the end of his bed. He is cranky, barely tolerant of the thermometer sticking out of the corner of his mouth. His skin has a yellow, jaundiced hue, and Will noticed a marked difference in his performance during the drill on Scots' Kopje the day before.

"This is ridiculous," he says through tight lips, but the pain in his stomach has given him a permanent wince.

"Shush, now," admonishes the nurse, attempting to get a read on his temperature. It is Hilde, to Will's chagrin. But she ignores him.

At the onset of his sickness, Mason awakened with a headache and cold chills. Hardy served him a cup of beef tea, but when that did not alleviate his condition, the corporal went in search of Will.

Hardy has it from a reliable source that A Company is to be included in a New Year's Day sortie, and this is the reason behind Mason's foul mood. Surely he will miss their first real engagement. But Will is envious, actually, not because he is afraid of the expedition, but because Mason will be left behind in constant contact with Claire.

"One hundred and three," Hilde announces, shaking the mercury stick. "That's up a degree from an hour ago."

The barn is substantially cooler than it is outside, and the heat began in earnest the day before, rising to one hundred and six by noon, but Mason's torso is glistening with perspiration even in here.

"Looks like you've got the fever. I'll get you some ice chips from the block house, but we're going to have to keep you for a while."

"No worries. I'll bag one for ya, mate," says Hardy, adopting the rather foolish parody of an accent he has picked up from his new friends in the Queenslanders.

"Please," Hilde groans on her way down the ward.

‡

Robert dreams of sand in his mouth and awakens choking, unable to move. It's a condition he has had since childhood, this temporary paralysis. Normally, if he remains calm, concentrates—on moving an eyelid, or his baby finger—his bodily functions return slowly, by increments. But he is panicked now, unable to breathe. His mind is trapped in the shell of him. He wants to call out to Will, to beg for help, but his tongue is lodged in the back of his throat.

In his dream, Robert was sinking into prairie, flailing about with his arms before the earth swallowed him whole. Sand poured through him as he passed layers of stone and silt. The evidence of a forgotten inland sea. He had been calling to Veccha across waves of prairie grass—calling to his wife—but she would not turn to face him. The roof of their sod hut was collapsed upon itself, and the windmill cranked and spun, unleashed from the pump below. When he tried to move, Robert found his boots already covered in loam. A moment later he was among the company of ichthyosauri, archaeopteryx, and tiny ammonite curls.

The first organs to return are his lungs. Oxygen spills in where the sand has passed, opening up grapes of starving areolae, and immediately he is a drowned man returned to the world. His voice is a shock of ragged electricity parting the air above his lips. When his eyes finally open, Robert believes he can see words on the skin of the tent from the scores of unsent letters beneath his bed. He coughs, and they disappear, leaving green splotches of erasure.

"You okay?" asks the young man across from him.

"I'm fine," Robert replies, without looking. Because he cannot yet turn his head.

‡

The Dutch town of Douglas is fifty miles north of Belmont. Somewhere between there and the British garrison, a Boer raiding party is hiding out, wreaking havoc on the rail lines and ambushing patrols outside Magersfontein. Colonel Pilcher had been lobbying his commanding officers for some time for permission to launch a series of sorties into Boer territory, and finally receives the go-ahead. After watching the Royal Canadians on parade, he chooses A Company to join a long list of Imperial and colonial troops on a New Year's Day sortie, dubbed Sunnyside. Will and Robert and Hardy are among the chosen who will accompany members of the Queensland Mounted Infantry, P Battery of the Royal Horse Artillery, the Imperial Mounted Infantry, the Royal Mounted Fusiliers and two companies of Cornwalls.

Will packs his haversack with hardtack, bread, and an extra bottle of water. He is only slightly nervous about the encroaching march. Worried more about missing Claire. He has steeled himself against the possibility of death during the last few weeks working with the injured from Magersfontein. But then he cannot really remember a time when he was truly afraid of death. Or at least of being killed. He has, in retrospect, always believed that he was somehow charmed, destined for a long life. He is, however, apprehensive about the metaphysics of death. About what happens when the candle is out. But it is only a vague fear, and he is often able to detach himself from it, like stepping out of his skin as he did on the morning the birds arrived. Or as he eventually did in the days following the labourer's rape and assault. His only concrete concern about the possible engagement ahead is his performance. Mason throws around words like *honour* and *glory* as though they are tangible, but Will isn't really sure what they mean, or that they apply to war as he understands it at all.

So as he steps into line with Robert, and as far from Hardy as he can manage, Will clears his mind and thinks only of Claire beneath a shade tree eating chocolate.

‡

The fevered have an aura about them, Claire thinks. An acuteness of being, similar to that of a morning after rain. They glow with unparalleled intensity and clarity.

Like typhoid, enteric fever is brought on by ingesting infected water or contaminated food. It can lie dormant in the body for up to three weeks before an outbreak. So neither Claire, nor the doctor at Belmont, has any idea how long Mason has been sick. One thing is certain, however. His case is already advanced by the time he is admitted. How he had kept up with the drills is a mystery.

Claire watches him from a distance. Mason is just one among the throngs of enteric cases, which now outnumber the wounded. His prognosis is good, however. This much Claire has gleaned from the staff doctor. But he will have to suffer through on aspirin until it passes. No other treatment is available.

His fever spiked earlier in the week, a day after the Canadians were sent out. He had been complaining the whole day previous about how unfair it was to be left behind, but by the time the troops were marching, he was oblivious. Tossing under wet sheets. Moaning about the heat one minute, shivering the next. In his moments of coherence, he is plagued by headaches. She sits by him then, when she can.

He has not eaten since the day before he was admitted, and after a week of such suffering his body is all angles. Protuberance of bone. The condition was, of course, made worse by periods of diarrhoea and even vomiting during the worst of it. He is too weak to stand even now, though the critical period has passed. He is confused. Floating in and out of consciousness. Levels of lucidity. When he speaks, there is no sense in it. She recognizes the child in him most then. For all his strutting bravado he is still not much older than a schoolboy, really.

Infection of the spleen and liver are always the danger with enteric. Intestinal bleeding in the most dire circumstances. But Mason is lucky. A week, maybe two, and he will be up again.

She tries to imagine what her parents might say about a man like Mason, about love. She believes that her mother knows a thing or two about longing. Claire has caught her staring out windows, lost. And yet it was her mother, as often as it was her father, who invited a parade of suitors home for dinner. Older men, for the most part. Men of property and means. But even the younger men, just back from the university or an apprenticeship in Melbourne—men with prospects—could not fulfill what her parents referred to as her "Romantic notions."

How many meals were spent listening to the awkward click of knife and fork on glass? How many more by the incessant drone of her suitor's virtues, devoid of any irony?

Claire is aware that what she expected from Mason's hospitalization did not occur. She is the victim of too many Victorian romance novels, she realizes, but somehow she expected a rapprochement. A convalescent affair. Brought on by what? she wonders now. Gratitude? Proximity? But she is not sure that he feels anything. And yet, she cannot think her parents might have been right to think her a foolish Romantic.

Perhaps she is being unfair. He is ill, after all. But, no. That is not it. As she watches his chest rise and fall—his slow return to normalcy and health—she realizes that her assessment has nothing to do with him. It is she who feels nothing. Nothing at all.

‡

The Boer are spotted by the mounted Queensland scouts just beyond a kopje near Badenhorstfontein. Will and the rest of the Little Green Devils ascend the nearby slope as an escort for P Battery, who are to arrange their guns in preparation for the engagement. Will's stomach is in a flurry, the way he felt before public speaking contests or his bit performance in last year's school play.

He can see the Boer riders entering the gulch where Colonel Pilcher hopes to trap them, but they are far beyond the reach of his Lee-Enfield rifle. It hardly seems possible to Will that they will comply with the British officer's predictions and ride unknowing into the ambush. Their wily reputation precedes them. However, the little line of horsemen plods carelessly along.

From this distance they are mere toys, and Will is shocked to discover that if he were required to fire down upon them now, he would be able to do so, without rancour, as though it were simply a game. A turkey shoot. It is only then that he understands the need for the protracted drills. His actions must be automatic and without thought. He is a good shot, and was told as much by Captain Bell at the Morris tube ranges aboard the *Sardinian*.

"Steady hands and slow trigger finger," he had commented.

The product of afternoon adventures with Mason as a boy.

Robert is ensconced behind a stone beside him, looking down the barrel of his own weapon. And yet, no matter how many times Will sees the man with a gun, he cannot help but find them an odd match. How does he feel? Will wonders. Is there any sense of hesitation in those soft hands?

Down the line, Will hears someone retch, followed by the sounds of rocks sliding as several others scurry to quiet the nervous soldier. The Vickers guns are in place, and the men await the order beneath a surreal calm. But then something happens. A skittish horse whinnies somewhere down on the veldt, and Will realizes that it is one of the Queenslanders' mounts.

The Boer pull up, already halfway into the pass. Their voices rise out of the gulch, and the first shot is fired. The lone bullet has time to echo and reverberate through the hills. The renegade horse enters the field riderless, and Will knows that somewhere on the plain below, an Australian rider lies dead. The ensuing response is deafening.

It is difficult to know if any of Will's shots fly true, but the rain of rifle fire from the assembled host, coupled with the guns of P Battery, is most definitely effective. Even from several hundred yards, it is clear that the Boer topple with their horses against the sandy plateau. The rear guard, not yet within range, turns and flees. But close to half of the party is trapped.

Without thinking, Will works the bolt action rifle with surprising fluidity, picking targets at random and not watching to see if they fall. Perhaps not wanting to see. However, during this action, and from the corner of his eye, he sees Robert staring down the barrel of his rifle, his hands frozen on the trigger. Will barely has the time to process this as he continues to work the bolt, scanning the valley floor.

The remaining Boer scramble into the natural fortress of the kopjes, ducking behind boulders, and struggling up the slopes in search of higher ground. It is an instinct for survival that drives their initial actions, an unwillingness to surrender. But Will can see, even from this early assessment of the battle, that the Boer cause is a hopeless one. The British advantage is overwhelming. Nonetheless, the two sides exchange fire long into the afternoon.

A runner delivers water to those men in the firing line, and for more than four hours Will holds his position. The Vickers guns pulverize the hillsides, until finally the Boer toss down their weapons and raise their hands in defeat. The British guns come to a stop in an erratic, haphazard fashion—anti-climactically, it seems to Will, after the sharp day's action. The last shots ring out like keys struck on a typewriter.

‡

The men plunder the Boer laager under the gaze of the Dutch prisoners. It is a final humiliation, though the farmers say nothing.

The actions of the British forces are against all regulations, but the officers are so pleased with the operation that they turn a blind eye. There is talk of pressing on into Douglas. Surely the town's defences are depleted after today's catch.

Will cannot bring himself to take from the cache, however. Instead, he finds a boulder in the shadows of a hill. Seated, he watches the men pick through overturned chests. Forage in cloth-covered wagons—the elongated carts used by the original *voertrekkers*. It is not a large camp, and there is little of any value beyond the team of eight oxen quickly adapted into the British ranks.

Clothing, he supposes—shirts and trousers—are the prize possessions. The wide-brimmed slouch hats are also popular, especially among the Canadians. Many of the British companies already have adequate protection from the sun with their puggarees. But Will and the other Canucks are burned scarlet about the neck.

Some men seek out kettles and camp utensils without considering the extra weight of transport.

The prisoners are brought in from the ragged kopjes behind the camp, and a few caught fleeing are marched in from the bushy plain. Gathered about a wattle Kaffir hut they stand or crouch, despondent—eyeing the British troops greedily drinking from their water cart.

On the far side of the camp between two stunted trees, a group of Australians divides up the slaughtered carcass of a sheep they discovered slung there.

During his observations, Will spies a body in the dirt. A tiny corpse. He stands to retrieve it, and discovers that it is a doll. A china harlequin. It is a surprising discovery here, and useless, really. But he decides to keep it. There is so little beauty here.

Veccha,

> *I need not explain fate to you, I'm sure. You, more than anyone, understand the razor thin arc of a man's life. However, I wonder what it would do to you, to see the end of that arc on a desert floor. To see it with your own eyes would be different, I think—different than some form of disembodied knowing.*
>
> *I understand now, as much as you, what lies in store for*

me. Perhaps I understand it even more now, though it stands in opposition to everything I've ever known, or thought I knew. You must forgive my ignorance, Veccha. We are creatures of habit. Where once I saw patterns, I now see only chaos. Things, Veccha, they begin to fall apart.

Yours,
Robert

‡

The better Boer wagons are recruited by command to carry the prisoners. The water cart as well is confiscated and sent back to Belmont. The rest of the camp is burnt. Supplies of straw are laid in under shattered wagons stacked with useless enemy ammunition and other camp detritus. The sound of the bonfires' erratic snapping reminds Will of the previous day's action, only now it seems even more surreal, as the troops lazily pull together their belongings, don their greatcoats, and sling their haversacks for the march ahead, oblivious to the violence of nearby gunfire—the crackle of potential death.

The grayscale before first light is eerie and strange to him, and the smell of charred wood and metal fills his nose.

In direct contrast to this scene, the first leg of the day's march is as pleasant as any morning stroll back home. Tramping along in a skirmish line of fours, the column makes good time to Rooi Pan. The men from the Niagara region even start to sing at one point in the journey, and although Will does not join in, he is lulled by the sound of their deep voices in the rising sun.

The first waypoint, a farmhouse, is well provisioned with two ponds, and they fall to filling their water bottles immediately upon arrival. The squat little homestead was recently inhabited but the troops find it abandoned when they arrive. It is rumoured to be the home of Piet Faber, one of the prisoners taken yesterday.

Colonel Pilcher calls the rest to an end after only half an hour, and all too soon Will is marching again, the morning's agreeable walk a distant memory as the sun crawls toward full height and bears its ferocious teeth. To make matters worse, the ground becomes sand beneath his feet and he, along with the entire infantry, struggles to make time and keep up with the mounted Queenslanders. The wagons too become swamped and those fortunate enough to have secured a spot on board are forced to dismount and push to keep the column moving.

Robert is one of these men, and when Will spies him shouldering a floundered cart, he jogs forward to lend a hand. For almost a mile, wordlessly, they push and slip along behind the supply wagon. But just being near the older man is reassuring to Will. Sensing the force of his determination, his almost animal sense of duty, relieves Will's anxiety over yesterday's engagement and Robert's behaviour throughout.

There is a general sense of relief among the troops as finally they attain the government highway which had been under construction by Boer labourers before the outbreak of war.

As a reward for his efforts, Will takes a place on the very wagon he forced through the desert and rests for a while, listening to the Negro mule drivers as they speak to their beasts over the clatter of the wheels on hard-packed stone.

In the distance a sugar-loaf hill indicates the low-lying ridge south of Douglas, and the disappearance of the sheltering kopjes.

Finally Will breaks the silence shared with Robert. "Shouldn't we be on alert?"

Robert turns his head like an ancient turtle. The look on his face, simultaneously dumb and intelligent.

"I mean, so far into the Territory and with Douglas just beyond?"

Robert cranes his neck backward to eye the chain of low hills. The whitewashed stubble on his chin harbours the incipient light of the sun. He breathes loudly through his nose. It could be a statement, or simply a sigh.

Either way, Will understands that his question is an unwelcome interruption upon whatever illusion the man has created for himself. He has forced him into the moment to consider their imminent future. But as Will should know, Robert would rather not think on that too much.

It is an ability Will wishes he could learn.

"The scouts," answers a voice behind them.

Will turns to discover a private from the Niagara company holding his knees to his chest, rocking with the motion of the mule-drawn cart.

"The Queenslanders have ridden ahead to look for an ambush." The young man, like Will, is blond and long-legged. He imagines having seen him before in camp or on the march, which is more than possible. But beyond a handful of close acquaintances, Will realizes that the army for him is a single mass, and that the anonymity of its soldiers is something Command encourages.

"Still," he says, no longer looking at Will, "there's a lot of brush out there. Plenty of places to hide."

Will looks out at the rolling, dusty landscape dotted now with brush and dwarf trees. The way they wobble in the heat. He looks at them hard, and notices at the same time that Robert does not.

‡

Beyond the low hills Will eyed earlier in the day opened a high plateau, and from that vantage he could see, through a blue haze, a valley. The town of Douglas lay somewhere amid that haze, shimmering just out of reach. Loyal to the Crown, it had been taken early by the Boer and held since the beginning of the conflict. Their little column was to be the town's relief.

Will considers the weary apathy of the soldiers around him and judges them very poor relief, indeed.

The road, still good, veers left sharply and begins its slow descent into the vale. Rising above the men to the west is a smooth sheer rockface, sloping perilously toward the same valley floor. Although it offers little room to hide, being so exposed and smooth, Will watches as five stick men lope along the spine of it, moving in a parallel line of descent as the main column of troops and wagons.

A moment later mounted Queenslanders blast past the stick men in a clatter heard by Will and the others even from that distance. The attitude of the line changes. Will sits up and watches the movement of the scouts as they all but disappear down the steep ridge. The guns are next, dragged off the road westward in the direction of the rumoured town.

But the heightened sense of alert slowly dies as the column wends its way unhurriedly down without incident.

Beneath the circuitous ridge of hills and rock the village finally materializes in the afternoon glare. It lies just beyond the butterscotch banks of the Vaal River, spread wide and thin, home to no more than a few hundred souls.

Will recognizes the Maxim guns that left the road earlier, now stationed in bas relief amid a tangle of bush and scrub brush, trained on the town below them.

The Queenslanders are almost invisible ahead as they ride spaced out toward the tiny village.

Will wishes for a spyglass and squints down the vale after them, kneeling in the back of the wagon. Even Robert looks over his shoulder, surveying the scene.

"Nothing but Union Jacks and red ensigns!" calls an officer perched atop his horse and staring through field glasses at the side of the road.

A murmur passes through the men, if not exactly a whoop. The Boer scouts must also have been doing their jobs, and ordered the garrison out rather than to stand and fight the superior force.

The first few homes they encounter are not unlike the Boer steads—low bungalows with shaded verandahs across the fronts. The flags, Will discerns, are home made, dyed and crudely stitched. An odd sight here in the Karoo so far from England. But weren't such anomalies just as present on Dominion Day in Manitoba? he thought. Weren't they just as far from home?

A face or two peers at the troops as the wagons roll in bumping over the roads, but most of the villagers await them over the canal in the town square. The municipal clock reads ten minutes after three when Will arrives. The Queenslanders have already run up a flag to match the town's and the initial cheering he'd heard coming over the bridge has disintegrated into a general hum of goodwill. Particularly in the direction of the town's hotel, where soldiers are already bellying up to the bar.

‡

Following the sunset parade, Captain Bell leads Will's company down to the banks of the river to bathe. The water is warm and swift, if a little off-colour. There is a race to see which soldier will be the first of the war to cross north of the Vaal. Will joins in, but only half-heartedly, unlike Hardy, who swims with all the skill of a drowning man, and who would forever be telling the troops back at Belmont about his exploits at the vanguard of the British forces.

Walking back through town in the still heat of the night, Will passes a titter of girls, not much younger than him, in full-length skirts. They are sharing a joke, drunk on the passage of so many foreign men through their little homes and lives. All in all, Will thinks, the Boer do not seem to have molested the settlement to any terrible degree. Although it is clear enough from their reception that the townspeople are happy with the British arrival.

Will knows from the crackle in the town square that already bonfires have been lit, and the unusable Boer ammunition is once again being tossed upon the flames. Like fireworks without the light show. In stark contrast to the morning's display, however, which had for Will the semblance of a medieval scorched-earth march, the evening fires are thick with celebration, and accompanied by song. And in spite of the Howitzers and the Maxims and the twelve-pounders facing the darkened drifts on the edge of town, happiness—a little bubble of hope—grows up around the village and Will does his best to maintain it. He breathes in deeply, afraid to see it burst.

‡

The next morning tears replace the laughter in the town square. Upon hearing that the army has no intention of leaving a garrison, that the entire column is set to leave that very day, more than half the villagers elect to leave their homes and travel on to Belmont. Once there, they will take the train to Cape Town and fall upon the charity of distant relations. Those who are not so lucky, or adventurous, choose to stay.

Will imagines the Boer infiltrators crouching north of the town, rallying at the sight of troop movement. Perhaps they are already resupplied and reinforced.

He and Robert help the departing families into the backs of the buck-wagons. Robert bends to pick up a little girl crying for her father already, who has decided to remain with the farm. He passes her through the air to the outstretched arms of her mother. Both men will be on the march today as a result of the civilian exodus.

Slowed by the additional bodies and stores, the troop train returns far later than expected to the twin pools of Rooi Pan, and a dust storm ruins their hasty meal. By four o'clock they are on the move again. The dust settles and the sun is covered by cloud. Fatigued and disorganized, the drawn-out parade of wagons, soldiers, and plodding civilians drags itself into the protective arms of the Thornhill chain of kopjes—a place called Cook's Farm that the troops used as a bivouac on their initial New Year's march north.

The next morning, the Cornwalls and half the force of Queenslanders are sent on to Belmont with a few remaining prisoners they pick up in Rooi Pan. The remainder of the troops, including Will's company, are ordered to rest while the officers prepare for a more orderly progression the following day.

The farmhouse, commandeered by Colonel Pilcher and his staff, buzzes with activity all day long, sending out messages, writing detailed reports of the Sunnyside affair, and gathering information about Boer troop movements to the north.

In contrast, the troops bathe in the farm's ponds, fraternize with the Douglas girls who have joined them on the march, or even sleep in the shade of the orchard.

It isn't until evening that a sense of foreboding creeps into camp. Rooi Pan, it is reported, has become the rallying point for twelve hundred Boer cavalry. The balance of the former Douglas garrison and reinforcements from raiding parties across the Orange Free State.

Will figures the British numbers to be just over three hundred, and in fact Hardy later informs him the exact number to be three hundred seventy. Two hundred of those are mounted on horses that have marched unreplaced and with little rest for almost a week.

Some thought is given to positioning troops and guns in the surrounding kopjes and awaiting troops from Belmont. Certainly the planned departure the following morning is impossible. Moving one hundred and fifty civilians ahead of a superior mounted Boer force is a death march.

Again it is Hardy who delivers the news to Will.

"We're to move out immediately. Go through the night. Pilcher's worried the reinforcements wouldn't reach us in time."

"How will we ever keep a group this size together in the dark?" Will asks.

"Better to take our chances out there, than to be trapped here and overrun."

‡

Men cling to the sides of overloaded wagons. Children, tired past all resolution, cry huddled amid the supplies.

The chaos of preparations is surpassed only by the ludicrous forced march. Clouds which rolled in during the afternoon now block all light from the sky. The drivers call out frequently to ensure the wagons stay in formation, but the cacophony of yelling and crying and disparate cursing of the troops is no more than an interference. Certain wagons become bogged down, forcing hasty evacuations and, in the worst cases, a redistribution of cargo, or outright abandonment.

"Where's the cavalry?" asks Will, out loud but to no one in particular.

"They're trying to set the pace," answers Robert.

The line of civilians and soldiers stretches so thin now, communications have completely broken down.

"Can you see the wagon ahead of us?"

Robert squints, but does not answer.

Suddenly Hardy is panting at Will's side, a pale ghost from the darkness. "We've lost the last wagon. The wheel came straight off."

His skin is moist with the exertion of running. Even in the dark, Will can see the pan-sized whites of his eyes.

"What about the refugees?"

"They're coming, mostly. On foot."

"Mostly?"

"A few of the men refuse to leave their possessions behind."

"Stop the wagon," Robert calls to the black driver. And a moment later it clatters to a halt.

"Won't we lose the rest of the train?" asks a woman over the edge of the buckwagon. Her voice is a high trill with fear in it.

"We ought to keep moving." A man's voice this time, anonymous from the far side of the cart.

Will's mind is racing. He stares off to the east from where Hardy just arrived.

"How far back?"

"Not far."

A short round colonist slides to the ground and joins the soldiers. "We can't wait for the others. The Boer horsemen could be upon us at any minute. You must get us to Richmond House." He is almost shouting.

"Quiet," Will hisses. And in the brief hiatus that follows, it becomes clear to everyone present that there are indeed horses in the distance.

"Cavalry?" asks the little man.

Will ignores him and addresses Hardy. "Go back and corral the stragglers."

Hardy turns, but then, as though remembering his rank he stops, hesitates. After a moment, he shakes his head and sets off.

Will brushes past the gentleman from Douglas and rounds the back of the wagon. "Robert, help me toss this cargo over the side. We'll make room for the others."

"Not my things," cries the woman on board. The child in her arms begins a low wail now, as well.

Then the first shots ring out, still some distance off. Robert scrambles into the wagon with Will. The woman passes off the infant to a male child, and even she aids the soldiers as they hoist the remainder of her life in Douglas into the sand.

"It's only scouts," says Robert, almost out of breath. "Otherwise they'd overrun us."

Another shot opens the night, just as Hardy and a handful of Canadian soldiers appear out of the black. The last of the refugees aren't far behind.

Will aims his rifle at the night and fires in return. The refugees and a few soldiers drop to the ground. A horse whinnies not far to the west of the wagon.

"Everyone up," says Will, extending a hand to the first of the colonists.

An instance of fear passes through the small band as two mounted Queenslanders gallop in from the opposite direction. They rein in for only a moment to assess the situation before hurrying off in the direction of the Boer.

A long half-hour passes with the soldiers exchanging gunfire periodically, the oxcart being driven ruthlessly over the haggard landscape, before Hardy spots the blazing lights of Richmond House farm in the vale below them.

It is close to three o'clock when their wagon rolls into the safety of the yard. The Queenslanders are just behind with frothing horses.

"I think the scouts have retreated," one says as he draws his horse in close to the wagon.

Another inquires, "Everyone safe?"

The overcrowded cart discharges its human cargo, and Robert leads the civilians to other transport.

Hardy slaps Will on the back. "Close one, eh?"

The fat man smiles, but already he is patting his breast pocket in search of a smoke.

Will wonders how long it will take them to return to Belmont, and when he will next see Claire.

‡

Mason is envious, but fit after more than two weeks in the infirmary. Hardy boasts to have single-handedly brought the Boer to their knees, but Will is evasive when questioned by his friend. Claire is polite and happy when Will visits her upon his return, but he senses a greater distance between them, and finds her too busy to meet with him on subsequent drop-ins.

One morning, later in the week, he sees her with Mason by the windmill just after rouse. Mason is leaning in over her shoulder with one hand on the tree by her head. Will knows it is Mason, because he has taken to wearing the Boer flop hat ever since the return of the Sunnyside sortie, the one Will stole for him that afternoon on Scots' Kopje. At one point during the conversation, she reaches out to touch his arm.

Will is crestfallen, and finds himself volunteering for extra duties to occupy his mind. Several times he pulls a picket with the night patrol, but Mason accompanies him on each shift, hoping to engage Boer spies in the surrounding kopjes. On two different occasions the soldiers find themselves pursuing a possible enemy, but on neither patrol do they actually exchange fire, much to Mason's chagrin.

Rumours of another expedition into Boer territory circulate among the men, but nothing materializes. Not even Hardy seems to know when the regiment will get its next shot. Will's mornings are often filled with drills, but when he can find nothing else to do in the afternoons, he tags along with Robert. He is more than happy to share in the man's silence now, and when he does choose to speak, his conversation is never about the war. Will learns about stabilized land mass, tectonic plates, and the continental drift. Robert tells him about the age of rocks and the persistence of time, but he does so in small packages of language broken by extended periods of quiet. The man, Will realizes, does not understand small talk. And that suits Will just fine.

‡

Every so often their drills are interrupted by freak dirt devils, dust storms that descend like fingers of wind and spread until the veldt is a blizzard of sand. The men break ranks and stumble back to their tents, using handkerchiefs and cloth caps to cover their mouths, shield their eyes.

For days after, Will finds himself chewing the grit from his food. The dust invades everything. He and Robert beat their blankets after every tempest and still their beds are filled with sand. Their water has texture.

When the men cough, frequently they spit up gobs of earth. Slowly, it seems, the veldt is determined to consume them. Will says this aloud to Robert one evening in the privacy of their tent. Outside the wind howls.

"It is only a matter of time," the older man replies.

And Will regrets having said anything at all. He turns in his bedroll. Tiny, insipid grains scratch at the small of his back.

‡

Claire runs into Will by accident one afternoon outside the station. She is on her way back from the shop with the papers from Cape Town, more than a week late. Sister Martha has afforded her the time now that the epidemic of fever is over. She has avoided Will since his return from Badenhorstfontein, and she cannot help but blush as they cross paths.

"Look what the cat dragged in," she says, attempting to sound aloof.

But the meeting is made all the more embarrassing by the young man's lack of clothing. The heat has persisted since after Christmas, and he is shirtless now, just back from unloading carts at the ammunition depot.

"Hi," he says, pale eyes blinking. She registers the difference between his body and Mason's. The gentler, almost feminine lines. And although she cannot say why, today she thinks of him as beautiful.

"I don't see you anymore," she says, but his face tells her that he is aware of how things stand.

"It's the bloody war," he says, borrowing her own expression.

"Walk back with me?" she asks, before she can stop herself.

"It's on my way," he smiles.

The quiet between them is something she could never share with

Mason. She remembers it from that first night along the same road, when her train had just arrived. And she is suddenly sorry for her poor behaviour in the last week. She can count on one hand the number of times she has seen Mason over the same period, and not one of them has been of his contriving. Hilde likes him less than Will. Says he flirts with all the nurses, but has nothing more to talk about than the war. Or himself. Of course, Claire can see it as well. Or at least she can see it now.

"Are you participating in the day of athletics?" she asks, breaking the silence.

Command has organized a day of general competition at the end of the week to ward off the unrest they sense brewing among the troops.

"No," he says. "Mason's the real athlete."

Claire senses an edge to the name, as though it were a rock in his mouth. "Then come out and watch with me," she says, and Will turns his blue eyes upon her.

"Sure," he answers after a moment's hesitation.

Somehow then, their hands brush in the regular swing of their walk, and Claire's heart skips at the contact, like the beating of caged wings. A moment later, their hands are joined, and she is shocked by this sudden and totally unexpected loveliness.

Uncle John,

Mason missed everything while he was on fire with enteric fever. He burned for days and days. I too marched into the desert surrounded by flames, or at least it felt that way under the unforgiving sun. That's where I found the enemy for the first time. As Mason dreamt only of water, I released death into a valley, and discovered it was easier than I'd ever imagined. Those who were not killed, I brought back in irons.

Please don't hate me, now.

Claire watched over Mason while I was gone She pressed cool water to his brow. Perhaps she even sang in the dead of night. But something has changed. It is I who need watching, now. Somehow she knows this, I suspect.

I am thirsty even after drink. It's much worse than I'd ever imagined. Worse now that there is some scrap of hope. I am, of course, referring to Claire. There will never be any hope for the war.

Yours,
Will

‡

The day of athletics is a roaring success, but no other regiment is able to compete with the Queenslanders. They have amassed more firsts than all of the others combined. The Royal Canadians take consolation in a distant second place. But the cross-country run is the day's final event, and A Company lays its hopes upon a recently recovered Mason. Almost everyone turns up for the race, which takes place in the early evening once the temperature has dropped. The course winds out around Enslin's Kopje, where the crowd will lose sight of the runners for a time, and ends with their reappearance in a downhill sprint to the finishing line.

Claire has been able to leave the ward for only short breaks during the day, but now she is free and standing next to Will. They have barely spoken since their walk back to camp days earlier. It has been confirmed that three companies of the Royal Canadians, including Will's, are to take part in a second sortie two days hence, and the drills have intensified as a result. This time, they will cross the border into the Orange Free State to pay a surprise visit to Commandant Lubbe's estate.

Will is confused by Claire's closeness and unable to concentrate on the preparations for the race. He wishes to reach out and touch her, just to reassure himself that she is really there, and with him. But he is not sure whether she meant to take his hand on the road at all, and is afraid the whole affair is a mistake. The Canadians are roaring a cheer for Mason as the runners take the line, and Claire looks back to Will, smiling. The squint of her green eyes infects him, and he joins in the chorus.

Mason looks hungry, almost angry with intensity. He is leaner than usual from his recent illness, even his smile has a terrible edge. Dark eyes brooding and hard. He has been this way since they were children, remembers Will. He could never understand the competitive psyche, but perhaps it only exists in those who can compete, he thinks.

When the captain raises the starting pistol, Claire reaches back to touch Will on the chest. Her head does not turn, but he can imagine the look of anticipation, the half-bitten lip. And he can feel the excitement through her. The pistol emits a barely audible pop in the din of the assembled fans, but it is loud enough to set the runners in motion. Mason is among the leaders. The crowd cranes and stands on its toes as the athletes race onto the veldt, and Will, who is taller than most, reports the standings to Claire, who loses them behind the sea of broad backs. Eventually they round the kopje and disappear entirely.

The course has been estimated at a mile and should take no more than a few minutes now that it has begun, but while the athletes are lost to the crowd, a calm befalls it as it anticipates their return over the hill.

"Isn't this exciting?" Claire beams, looking upward into Will's face.

And he is not sure what is more exciting to him at that moment, the race or her upturned gaze.

A moment more and the crowd cries out. Two men crest the hill almost simultaneously. One is a private from the Queenslanders, evidenced by the shouting from that contingent, and the other is Mason.

In spite of the war and its effects upon the friends, its delineation and its clarification of the differences between them, Will cannot help but recognize the artistry in Mason's movements. The perfect tilt of his body and the precision of his form.

In the last one hundred yards, the athlete explodes, and what has been a close race disintegrates in a final burst of speed that has even the British regiments in a frenzy. When Mason crosses the finish line with his hands aloft and triumphant, Will cannot contain his elation.

And as his friend is hoisted by a chorus of men, Claire turns and kisses Will.

‡

"My wife can see into the future," Robert tells Will.

It is well past lights out, but neither man is sleeping. Will thinks only of Claire, and Robert is obviously lost in his own entanglements.

"Or at least people think she does, and she has convinced herself that it is so."

Will is just as stunned by the man's candour as he is by the unusual nature of his confession.

"She told me not to come here," he continues. "Not out of love—it has never been that way between us, I'm afraid—it was more like a warning. A forecast." Robert's voice is devoid of emotion. He might well be pondering the nature of alluvial flood plains. It is the same tone he uses on their walks.

"Did she say you were going to die?" Will's voice cracks in the transmission after hours of disuse. He is worried about Robert. Stupefied by his latest revelation.

"Not in so many words," answers Robert. "She would never consciously transfer the burden. Not unless she were asked." A long pause ensues into which slinks silence like a cat. "I could never ask," he says finally. "But it was enough to know that she would rather I not enlist."

The silence. Will reels with the need to fill it.

"A terrible burden," says Robert, breaking the spell, before turning to the wall and settling in to another long night.

Will wants to press him further. It is the most personal revelation Robert has ever shared with him. And he couldn't imagine anything stranger. But he knows the man too well after the last few months. His body language suggests that the matter is closed.

He isn't sure what to think about this clairvoyance. He isn't even sure such a thing is possible. The fact that someone so rational, however, could treat the subject plausibly is compelling to Will.

And in retrospect he can now reconcile it with something else Robert said to him out on the veldt. He'd been talking about a culture's need to preserve its past, leave something for future generations.

"We're the only animal who thinks of the future this way," he said. "We're the only animal aware of our own demise."

So in some way, whether Will believes in clairvoyance or not, he must agree that all men know the future to some extent. All men know that we someday come to an end.

And who could be more aware of this end than a soldier?

"It's rather noble that we press on in spite of that knowledge. Don't you think?"

Robert adds that a long time after, so that Will isn't immediately sure of what he is speaking. As a result, he doesn't answer.

‡

Will is marching back from Scots' Kopje when he sees them. At first he suspects another dust storm. A black cloud descends upon the camp from the north, moving over the hills like water. But then he recognizes the cloud.

"Locusts," says Mason, who plods next to him.

Will has seen similar swarms of grasshoppers over the prairie around Portage. The locusts are worse.

Will intended to speak with Mason about what Robert told him the night before—or possibly the kiss from Claire—but the distance between the two now seems so unbridgeable that secrets alone can fill the gap. And the arrival of the locusts kills any further chance that they might speak.

They hit A Company like a bombardment of shell fire, crashing into soldiers who take cover and cower. Will takes a direct hit in the left cheek and cringes under the pain. He crushes the culprit beneath his boot as it drops to the ground in front of him. The sting of his wound welts immediately.

Mason grunts and Will suspects a similar assault. The worst of the cloud rushes past and dissipates in under a minute. The carcasses of dead bugs and stragglers remain, carpeting the veldt in little black turds. The soldiers rise, dazed, and trundle back to camp, nursing their wounds.

Since their arrival in South Africa, the Canadians have battled the natural world with far more ferocity and frequency than they have any party of Boer. Were it not for Sunnyside and the trains of wounded from Magersfontein, Will would be ready to believe the war was a sham—part of an absurd experiment in deprivation.

Just yesterday, he and Mason took turns delousing each other, and their clothes. Searching through strands of hair for tracks of white eggs and elusive, transparent lice. Squeezing the life from their resilient shells, between cracked fingernails caked with earth. An agonizing process that ultimately failed. Already, Will is scratching anew. At night he can feel them at work in his uniform, crawling over his skin. The entire army is infested.

The exoskeletons of the locusts burst beneath his combat boots on the way back to Belmont. There is no avoiding them.

‡

Will cannot sleep. He has not slept well in days in spite of the exhaustion he gathers to himself like a blanket. He suspects the same of Robert, who tosses and turns on the mattress beside him every night. Sometimes the man rises and leaves the tent for hours at a time. Will says nothing to him. Robert carries knowledge he cannot comprehend. Ironically, he is also the cause of Will's insomnia.

Not even the surprise of Claire's new intimacy can make him forget the Sunnyside sortie, or Robert's new intimations. He used to be able to compartmentalize and detach himself from things. A sort of mental defence mechanism. But there is no denying that he might have killed someone in the past week. It is something he cannot escape. But the most difficult part of this realization is that he had a choice. Like Robert, he did not have to fire into the canyon that day. Consequences might well have followed such inaction, and perhaps even Robert will one day be caught, but Will had a choice nonetheless. What frightens him the most as he lies alone in the darkness of another African night is the ease with which he made that decision. Subconscious abeyance. Thought without thought. How easy it is to kill, he thinks. And yet Robert did not.

Each time Will closes his eyes, the parade of defeated Boer marches past him. Their bearded faces masking the misery their sloping shoulders belie. Some of them newly brotherless, or fatherless. Or worse. And it is perhaps Will who visited this misery upon them. And what about the black boy? Where has he gone? As much as he craves the sleep that eludes him, Will feels as though insomnia is the smallest penance possible. For if he is honest with himself, given the choice a second time, he will not hesitate to kill. It is a decision Will knows to be true, yet he cannot comprehend its inevitability.

He can forgive Mason his blind observance to duty and the propaganda of the war machine. His friend is deluded. But Will's understanding of the war grows sharper with each mile they march into the desert. Robert has the courage and ability to act with conscience in the face of a terrible portent, real or imagined. But it is not courage to act that Will is wanting. It is the convictions upon which to act that he lacks. And this is why he cannot sleep.

‡

Claire regrets having confided in Hilde the moment her news is out. The two are sharing a cigarette underneath the same shade tree where Will gave her chocolate. Smoke explodes from the young nurse's mouth, followed by an exclamation that Claire suspects is meant to be a derisive laugh.

"Not The Bump!" she says, too loud.

Claire hushes her with a movement of her hand. "Don't call him that," she chastises her friend. "And for God's sake, keep your voice down."

Hilde passes the half-finished cigarette back to her, chuckling softly and coughing on the remains of her last drag so that her whole body is involved in the motion. Claire raises the fag to her own mouth and looks away.

"Oh, I'm sorry. But honestly, Claire, what did you expect me to think?"

Claire exhales. She's being unfair, she realizes. Worse than unfair. Because the truth is she's not even sure what she's doing herself. Or how she feels about it. Claire shakes her head and passes the cigarette back to Hilde. "I don't know. I guess I was hoping you'd make me feel differently about the whole thing."

"I mean, sure, he's fetching. I'll give you that. But he's only a boy. And what a mope. The only person it rains on in South Africa is Will."

The two women share a laugh that releases the tension of only moments before. A column of Tommies marches past on the road beneath them, casting long shadows on the lawn. It is the end of the day, and they've fallen out of step. Stray fragments of conversation rise from their tired ranks. Some smartass whistles his appreciation of the nurses. The men joke and jostle each other.

Hilde blows them a kiss and then turns back to Claire. "What happened, anyway? Just last week you had your knickers in a knot over the other one."

Claire shoves the other woman backward into the grass. "I did not," she lies. "Besides, it's not like I set out for this to happen. Why do you think I'm telling you about it?"

"So you won't mind if I have a go at him then?" says Hilde, rubbing the last of the cigarette out. "Bloody handsome little fellow, that Mason. Even if he is a bit of a tease."

Claire pushes her again, only this time Hilde grabs her arms and the two women topple over. And for a moment, they forget all about both of the men and dissolve into laughter.

‡

In his dreams, fitful moments of near sleep in a parade of sleepless nights, Will hears the screaming of their horses. And even though he knows it is imagined, that he could not possibly have heard such a thing from that distance and above the noise of the guns, it is more real to him than waking. The hail of lead and the drubbing of the Vickers guns' dumb assault rains down on the Boer ponies as they plod into the canyon unsuspecting.

Will sees the bullets crash into the withers, split limbs, and shatter bones and joints, in a spray of purple blood. The shrill whinny, filled with fear, seems an almost ludicrous response to the appalling damage, a sound incapable of expressing the full tenor of outrage and injustice. In these dreams there are no riders, and the British guns have no counterpart. The slaughter is casual and absolute. And even though he is revolted with his own actions, he does not let up.

When it is over, he scrambles down the hillside to walk among the twisted bodies, pistol drawn. Like this, he wades through fallen horses, killing anything that moves. The periodic pop and echo of his gun—its lonely sound—is worse than all the thunder of the regiment. It's enough to wake him every time.

‡

Robert remembers the wagons arriving at the end of their laneway, just after first light. It was a Sunday. Their first in the sod cabin of his own construction. A farmhouse, supposedly. Though he knew little about farming. He was dazed by the wagons' arrival, and completely unprepared for what their passengers sought. All of them would have awakened before dawn to arrive so early in the day. He suspected news of a hostile Indian tribe, a natural disaster. He suspected—he knew not what.

But Veccha knew. He watched her, in silence, minister to the small flock as a priest or a shaman might expect to do. He was awed by it, yes. But more than that, he was repulsed. The process of Veccha's spiritual meddling was preposterous. A parlour game from rich society matrons, or back-alley charlatans.

And so he forbade it. His first and only domestic decision as a husband. Afterward, he feared her. Visited her at night only when the physical need drove him beyond rationality. And even then, he was ashamed of himself.

But South Africa has changed him. The thin line between the living and the dead has never seemed so palpable. For the first time, he can see the thread of his own narrative, as he imagines Veccha can perceive the same thread in others.

He can imagine a man like himself, years from now, dusting his bones from the veldt. Attempting to pick up the same thread where he left it off.

‡

The first job of the British war mongers was to demonize the enemy. Will remembers the stories about the Boer slavers as terrible and cruel. But outrage over black whippings and torture would not be enough to spur the Empire on to war. The pressmen needed stories of civilian massacres, unjust executions, and the murder of their own countrymen for daring to surrender. The newsreels turned out fictional stormings of Red Cross tents, imaginary terrorist bombings, killed women and children on passenger trains.

But the most difficult task for the propagandists, by far, was the transformation of the beloved Uncle Kruger—known to his own people as "Oom." In the guise of political cartoons, the fat little Boer became a ruthless and decadent tyrant. A beer-swilling backwoods bandit hoisted into power through corruption and villainy, whose insatiable and sinful appetites knew no bounds.

And in the end, the public swallowed the bait. England and those who paid tribute to her beat the war drum. Men like Cecil Rhodes provided an influx of capital to support the venture, and colonial politicians cut a path to the motherland. But most importantly, young men like Will and Mason enlisted in droves. After all, what is a war without soldiers?

‡

When Will arrives, a small crowd has already gathered to witness the stag beetles fight to the death. They look like dark knights locked in ancient battle. Their black heads wield large burgundy mandibles the shape of Turkish scimitars. And their abdomens are covered in black metallic exoskeletons that shine like armour. The men have devised an arena in the belly of a slop bucket. Each time one of the beetles makes an attempt to flee, his legs slip on the smooth surface of the metal cage. This particular species is unable to fly, and is thus perfect for this form of entertainment. A Scottish soldier calls them rhinoceros beetles, but Will is unsure if this moniker is of his own devising or whether it is the proper name. Hardy runs the odds and collects the bets. Anyone with a beetle can enter.

Will discovers a large Canadian from D Company squaring off against one of the Shropshires. The beetles are similar in size, but there is perhaps a slight edge to the Tommy's entry. The crowd is not large but zealous in its enthusiasm, which only draws in more onlookers as the fight progresses.

"Wilson's undefeated," says a soldier Will's age, as though to fill him in on the drama. "That's Wilson," he adds, pointing to the man from D Company, in case Will is uninformed.

He notices Mason bent over the far side of the bucket. He is clearly cheering for Wilson. But the number of British regulars outstrips the Canadian's fan club, transforming him from champion to underdog, in spite of everything.

The beetles grapple with their front legs, which look like strings of tiny black pearls from the joint down, terminating in a two-pronged claw. The upper leg appears much more dangerous, with hook-shaped plates running back toward the abdomen. But this wrestling is not as deadly as the powerful jaw movement of the mandible.

The objective, thinks Will, seems to be a throw or reversal, brought on by the legs, so that the opposing beetle can stab its mandible into the softer underside of his opponent. A moment after he reasons this, the soldier confirms as much.

"It's not always the bigger beetle that wins," he says over his shoulder, not daring to take his eyes off the contest. "Sometimes the smaller one gets underneath the jaws and delivers a stiff uppercut."

True to form, Wilson's bug proves to be the more pugnacious, outmanoeuvring the larger beetle, but failing each time to finish him off. In fact, Will misses the eventual death blow, as the crowd leans in shouting, after the larger bug is thrown. The Brits curse their luck. A few Canadians slap Wilson on the shoulder. And Hardy pays out. The better half goes to the champion.

Will sticks around as the majority mope off, and he is surprised to see Wilson gather his beetle gingerly in cupped hands. He marches back toward his tent, sheltering the animal as one might shield a flame from the wind.

But more interesting than the man's tenderness, thinks Will, is that the beetles chose to fight at all. The bucket offered plenty of room for both.

‡

Will is beginning to understand that there are different types of silence—nuances, moments filled with things unsaid; times when there is nothing to be said. Absence. Silence like a vacuum. On Scots' Kopje this morning, he experienced the latter—a Boer hand rotted to bone almost. It protruded from the red earth like a final salute. Or perhaps it was raised in supplication, a last prayer to end this horror.

A rare storm the night before must have washed clear the silt of his shallow grave. Robert was no more than ten yards above Will, head down, poking in his own patch of dust. For what? Will wonders. He could flag the man's attention without lifting his voice. But then, Will has nothing to say. While he watches the misshapen salute, a beetle crawls from the faded cuff, sated on flesh. And he understands then that Robert too would say nothing. Language would be a far too civilized response.

When he tries to relate the story later, to Claire, he encounters the same paralysis. Only the silence has a new timbre. Each of them walks with a mouthful of words. A masticated dialogue without release. He wants to tell her many things, but Claire's silence is like a wall he cannot scale. He would begin with, "When I was a boy …," or "In my uncle's shop …" But somehow stories seem irrelevant here amid the death and the waiting. There was a moment, though, when he might have told her everything. On the road back from the rail station, perhaps. Or, after she kissed him. He isn't exactly sure, but he knows there was a moment, and that now it has gone. He is amazed at how quickly she slips away from him, when only days before he had such hope.

He would like more than anything to be behind her eyes as they pace out the camp perimeter in shared abstinence. To search silent thoughts. Feast on them.

‡

The column of soldiers moves through the eastern kopjes in a direct line to the border. It has not rained in a month and the sand twists in funnels around them, but above the sky is choked with clouds. The South African winter approaches. A Company is joined by the men from London, Ontario and the maritime city of Halifax. Mason is still riding high on his victory, and doubly pleased to be in the field for the first time since he left home.

The Canadians are part of a much larger sortie into Boer territory. P Battery of the Royal Horse Artillery, the Queensland Mounted Infantry, as well as the Cornwalls and the Munster Fusiliers are all strung out like a lethargic snake moving through the red sand. At Blaauboschpan Colonel Otter orders the men from Ontario to stand down. The column is still three hours' march from its intended destination and water is already scarce. B Company divides its extra canteens among the two remaining companies. Will takes a proffered flask from a Stratford man he's seen hanging around Hardy's tent, and then he and the rest of the Ontarians turn about-face and return to Belmont. The intent of this sortie, as Will understands it, is to rattle Commandant Lubbe by paying a visit to his home. Intelligence reports from the British scouts have large numbers of Boer riders coming and going daily.

All the marching he has done since his arrival in Cape Town, however, is beginning to show in Will's boots. The toes are scuffed and beaten. The soles are almost worn slick. He slips more than once on the rocky road through the Orange Free State. It is amazing to

Will that anyone would choose to live out here. Beyond small patches of prickly bush and tracks of hot sand, there is nothing to attract a homesteader or to endear the landscape to him.

Will swirls the remaining water in the bottom of his original canteen before swallowing a portion. To his left, Mason looks as though he is on parade. His alert demeanour puts the rest of the regiment to shame as they trundle through the heat of another African afternoon. His eyes shift in their sockets as he scans the open plateau and the distant blue kopjes for signs of the enemy. In his vigilance, it is Mason who spots Lubbe's farm first, and points it out to Will, flickering like a white flame on the baked horizon.

Moments later, an order is issued further up the line and the Queenslanders kick their horses into motion, shooting out on all sides to scout the destination in advance of the army's arrival. As the main body of the sortie approaches, Will can make out the small house stationed atop a low hill. It is surrounded by tall shade trees, and he can just discern the skeleton of a windmill pumping water from the burnt earth. The first of the Australian scouts returns as the marchers breech the outlying line of fencing, and word travels back down the column until it reaches Will and Mason. Three Boer were seen fleeing north into the distant kopjes.

Mason swears. But Will feels a sense of relief. His capabilities have already been tested and, unlike his hot-headed friend, he is not in a hurry to put them into action a second time. On orders from Colonel Otter, the regiment disperses into the yard.

Lubbe's house is a brick bungalow with a fine stone verandah. The trees protect it from the sun, which is now slowly burning its way through the cloud cover. Mulberry bushes crowd the front walkway and under the eaves. East of the house is a pomegranate grove. The farm is tidy to a fault, sectioned off with piled stone walls and enclosures. A barn and a henhouse stand west of the main home. And to the rear of the bungalow, there is a suite of servants' quarters.

The Cornwalls, who are detailed to search the barn, discover a cache of rifles and lyddite, trays of bullet castings. Immediately, they smash the weapons and confiscate the explosives. Will watches the men as they hoot and laugh, beating the guns against the hard-packed earth.

Hardy scurries over to interrupt the action with news from inside the home.

"They're interrogating the Kaffir slaves," he tells them, "over veal and rice."

"What are you talking about?" quips Mason.

"We've crashed a war council," he smiles. "The table's already been set, and now Otter and Blanchard and the other British officers are sitting down to fresh coffee and a full-course meal."

Just then, a Canadian soldier yells up to the house.

Mason spits, "Boer!"

Will follows the train of his friend's eyes. Sure enough, a small dust cloud blooms on the horizon. Seconds later, a British officer standing in the doorway of the bungalow orders the men to spread out along the stone enclosures at the edge of the lawn. The man is joined a moment later by the full contingent of officers, some still sporting napkins in their collars. Some of the Cornwalls move toward the stone wall, but most of the men look out over the yard, shading their eyes and pointing at the approaching force. The commanders pass around a pair of shared field glasses.

A sergeant steps off the porch and repeats the last order with authority. Will and Mason rush to the fence line and take up their positions. Men stumble in beside them, laying their rifles on top of the stones for support. The army is too far off for a shot, but nonetheless, Will also places his carbine in line. He can hardly believe that the Boer would ride up to the front door knowing that the British force was in place, and he says so to Mason, who is staring intently down the barrel of his Lee-Enfield.

"They're probably stragglers from the war council," he says in an unnecessary whisper. "Late for dinner."

A handful of Queenslanders are sent out on horseback to identify the approaching troops. A few moments of tense anticipation follow as Will watches the horsemen shrink into the distance. But to his surprise they do not pull up as they near the foreign riders.

"What the hell?" Mason breathes.

And then two of the men turn about and ride out front of the advancing regiment.

"They're Aussies," someone yells from further down the yard. "Look at their bloody hats." This provokes a whoop from the assembled Queenslanders.

Will can feel the adrenaline rushing away from his neck and into his shoulders. But Mason raises his head, confused. His furrowed brow scanning those closest to him for answers.

"Not Boer," Will smiles. "They're Australian troops."

The Victoria Mounted Rifles ride up through the yard to cheers, dismounting before the bungalow. The conjoined troops spend the night at Lubbe's enjoying the farm's fine stores as they exchange battle tales and information. Mason, thinks Will, is the only one who seems unhappy with the day's outcome.

‡

Dear Father:

I know my decision to leave Albury has been a great disappointment to you and to Mother. That you wished to shield me from the ills of the world is admirable, and now that I am removed in both time and space, I can see the wisdom of your intentions. But you also said that you expected more for me in life. I can only suppose what 'more' entails. A husband, perhaps. A wealthy farmer, or a merchant friend from Melbourne.

But my rejection of that life—departure—is as much your

doing as it is my own pig-headedness. In seeing me through an education at Melbourne's Methodist Ladies College, you have opened a world of new possibilities. And though I am willing to admit that South Africa may not have been the best available possibility, I must tell you that it is 'more.' More than the life you planned for me.

I am aware that you think I have squandered Nana's bequest. Given the right investments, it might well have kept me comfortable into spinsterhood, I know. But this experience has been the crowning achievement of my education. And I will always have my abilities. You had your start in life with nothing more. And we are more alike than any of us is willing to admit.

I write to tell you that I am safe, Father. That my work here is necessary. I trust you will come to believe, as I do, one day, that is more than enough.

Claire

‡

A company is given the day off, following its successful sortie, and Will is left to his own devices. Mason disappeared into the nearby kopjes just after lunch and, uncharacteristically, Will has not gone to the field hospital to look for Claire. Instead, he sits on the front lawn beneath the shade of the tall trees watching the men from B Company as they plod out onto the veldt for their afternoon march. Half-heartedly, he searched for Robert earlier, hoping perhaps to gather stones with him, if only to give himself something productive to do, but the man did not want to be found. Now Will is bored, with only his thoughts to entertain him.

Will has not received any particular commendation for his

soldiering since his arrival in South Africa, nor does he believe himself deserving of such; however, he has not been particularly berated for poor soldiering either. In the eyes of Lieutenant Blanchard and his other commanding officers, he is no doubt anonymous. But somehow he feels as though his anonymity is exactly what those officers are looking for. Will is a functioning instrument of war. He follows orders and he carries out his work to the best of his ability—no matter how banal the employment. Soldiering would not be his career of choice. And if he is honest, enlisting was not his idea. He was not in search of adventure, nor was he particularly worried about the state of the Empire. But then, clerking in his uncle's grocery would not be his ideal career either. And university, his original plan for this year, was simply a logical extension of the work he was doing in high school. Accounting and business are not passions for Will. He wonders now if he has ever been passionate. And Claire crosses his mind briefly. But that is not the sort of passion he means.

Will is thinking about direction. Ambition. He does not harbour any illusions of grandeur, so he cannot be disappointed with the war in the way Mason is. Equally true is that the war is not keeping him from anything more pressing or important. The suspended animation of this conflict is but a reflection of his own stasis. And to this stasis he is lucky enough to bring a work ethic imbued in him by his uncle. It would never occur to Will not to do things properly.

Unfortunately, he suffers from bad dreams. And therein lies the rub.

‡

Watching the Gordon Highlanders play football is akin to watching Mason run. The men from A Company are shipped out unexpectedly to Gras Pan in the first week of February. The small camp is only seven miles north of Belmont, but the march is murderous. Will's socks have all but disintegrated, leaving his feet open to blisters.

The only good thing about the move is the Canadians' reunification with the Gordons. At first, Will is shocked by the regiment's reduced numbers, and for the first time since the ambulance trains arrived at Belmont, the devastation of Magersfontein is a quantifiable reality for him. However, the Scots' welcome is so boisterous and genuine that he can feel nothing but elation. A radical change of mood after the long march. The bivouac from Belmont was so quick that he was forced to say goodbye to Claire in the middle of the ward. An awkward affair under the gaze of Hilde and the other nurses bustling back and forth. Rumour of a move for the medical staff was afoot as well, though no timeline or location had been established. Only once since Mason's race day had he been alone with Claire, and the prolonged hiatus of intimacy was evident as he fumbled for words. The march, however, had given him more than enough time to stew over it, so the atmosphere of celebration at the Gordons camp was a welcome relief.

On the morning of the second day, the Highlanders challenge the Canadians to a football match on a pitch of their own devising. The event is well attended by both sides, and even Will elects to participate in spite of the state of his dogs. Taped and bandaged, he chases down the ball for the Canucks in the backfield, only to be outwitted and outplayed the majority of the time. But he is not alone. The game quickly disintegrates from contest to demonstration on the part of the Gordons, who turn the sport into an art. The Scots, who are neither faster nor more athletic than their Canadian brethren, simply out-finesse them. The ball rarely escapes the Canadian half unless by way of a desperate clearing kick from the keeper, and then it is quickly picked up by the Gordons' halfbacks and paraded deep into the Canadian end again. It would be frustrating for Will, were it not for the magic of their spirited play. Daring passes, incredible footwork, and deadly accurate shots hold Will in awe. It lifts him out of the humdrum of the war and for a moment everyone present forgets about the Boer.

With only minutes remaining in the game, the Canadian coach calls for a substitution, and brings on a small blond-haired boy who must have stowed away on the *Sardinian*, given his height. Will has all but given up. Choked with want of air he makes only fleeting attempts to track down the Highland strikers. But in an odd twist of events, he manages to trap his man in the corner, forcing a bad pass which is picked up by an opportune halfback and relayed to the blond boy, who is already on the move. The Scottish fullbacks, who have been dallying for most of the game, are caught flat-footed as the boy catches the ball on his foot in mid-run, splitting the defence.

The sidelines erupt as he charges in alone on the Gordons' net, trailing three Highland fullbacks behind him. The Canadian team surges forward, as if by moving they can urge him on. Even Will is streaming up the right side of the field, well behind the play. Soldiers in the crowd are waving the boy forward, Royal Canadians as well as Highlanders. When the keeper leaves his box to cut short the boy's advance, he is taken by surprise. In a move more typical of the Gordons' level of play, the boy flips the ball up and over the sliding figure of the keeper, whose eyes widen as it passes over his outstretched fingers and into the empty space behind him. Three steps later, the boy traps the ball on the run and volleys it before he can be tackled by the closest defender. It passes through the upright posts as though guided by an outside force.

The Highlanders are so shocked by the last-minute development, and the Canadians so charged by their unexpected success, that the game dissolves into pandemonium. Will helps his mates hoist the blond boy into the air and carry him off the pitch triumphant. The only Canadian goal makes it a final of four to one.

‡

Robert watches the match with the sort of clinical detachment that angered his wife. He envisions her smouldering silently, unaware, perhaps, that she is upset, and certainly unsure why. But he knew.

People always frightened him, even as a child. Scientific

observation made an ideal career in light of this. The only time he was forced into confrontation was during the grant application process with the Royal Geographical Society. His lack of social refinement was never more evident than then. And it explains the meagre offerings that came his way over the course of his career. A poorly financed expedition to Ayers Rock. An even greater underfunded project on the Canadian frontier where, completely out of character, he met a woman and married her.

The random tumbling of his life makes it difficult for Robert to believe in fate. To understand his wife's clairvoyance. But then, the mystical management of the war, which finds him seated on a hillock observing a match of football in the desert, is part of some master plan, isn't it? And seemingly just as random.

He thought to eliminate such haphazardness from his life by devoting himself to rocks. To fossils. To the static. But all this was a delusion. Part of a paradox he is still working through. The world changes irrevocably; the world moves in cycles. His path is random; his path is set in stone. His passage has a purpose; his passage is anonymous.

Just then, a blond boy fresh from the sidelines takes the ball in alone. The crowd bursts like a rain cloud, and anything is possible.

‡

The return march to Belmont from Gras Pan is as unexpected as their bivouac only days earlier. All the men grumble audibly under the watchfulness of their officers. Mason is as loud as anyone. Even Robert looks weary, as he sits spread-eagle on the floor of their tent, shoulders sloped forward. Although he says nothing in response to the news, he does sigh and blow air through his lips. Will noticed the man's difficulty during their move north. He and several others had dropped back, and eventually, out of the formation. Will watched for him later as he came in with the stragglers after dusk. It is not uncommon to lose people on a march, but Robert did not seem to recover, even after the rest at Gras Pan.

Will has ceased to question the vagaries of military organization altogether. He views it instead as an elaborate dance. A medieval waltz through the desert with turns and promenades that he need only follow, if not understand. He is, however, happy to learn that the march is to take place at night, by moonlight. This way, the troops will avoid the punishing sun. His last night march was marked by the chaos and disarray of a retreat. This one promises to be less harrowing, if no less exhausting.

Only a mile from Gras Pan, the Canadians encounter a regiment of Gloucesters and Staffords marching north. The silence of that great lumbering body impresses him as the columns pass each other like ships slipping through anonymous waters.

Mason marches on Will's right. Robert has already fallen back, again. Will stares into the faces of the passing soldiers until he makes eye contact with a Tommy.

"Canadians?" the man shouts.

"Yeah," Hardy answers in his place. Will must turn his head to follow the British soldier.

"Three cheers for the Canucks," he bellows. And the column raises its collective voice.

The booming response is almost spiritual in the emptiness of the night—a Gregorian chorus, followed again by silence.

In spite of his disintegrating intimacy with Mason, Will is warmed by one aspect of his soldiering in South Africa. And this is it. The impromptu brotherhood that only increases with their proximity to danger.

‡

Will's relief upon arriving in Belmont following the night march is cut short when he realizes the field hospital and its staff have decamped in his absence.

"Gone north," an Aussie responds to his inquiry. "There's a push to relieve Kimberley. Fighting in Jacobsdal, or some such."

"They've taken our girls!" Mason shouts when Will returns to his tent. Hardy is there as well. Robert appears to have arrived only moments before. His pack lies in the middle of the floor, and he is still wearing his greatcoat.

"I just found out," says Will. He can tell from Mason's jocular tone that something is up. He was silent throughout the march, brooding over their return to this backwater, and now he is smiling with Hardy.

"Don't lose any sleep over it," Mason adds. "We'll be joining them before long."

Hardy interjects, "They've cornered Cronje's men south of Kimberley. Command is tightening the noose."

Will allows the two of them to drone on as he joins Robert on the floor. He has a terrible knot in his stomach. His throat hurts. He remembers the same feeling as a boy when Elizabeth Schuler's parents were moving away at the end of the summer, to live in the city. She had been his sweetheart through public school. He felt as though someone had punched him then. It was a similar sensation now. He knows that he is being ridiculous. That there is really very little between him and Claire, and that the possibility of battle in the near future should overshadow an almost adolescent heartache. But he feels awful nonetheless.

"What do you say, Will?" Mason asks, oblivious to the hurt.

Will pretends he does not hear and turns his face to the wall.

‡

Lord Roberts pays a visit to Belmont a day after the Canadians return. Mason and Hardy fight their way through the crowd at the railway siding in order to get a glimpse of the general. Kitchener is with him. Will could not imagine a more physical antithesis. Roberts, for instance, would not have qualified for the Canadian ranks, his stature is so diminutive. Kitchener, on the other hand, would have placed among the tallest of their regiment.

Mason and Will had been listening to Hardy swap stories with a British soldier all morning in anticipation of the commander's arrival. The Brit had served under Roberts in Khartoum. And not to be outdone, Hardy created exploits of his own in the Yukon under Sam Steele. Only Roberts' arrival could quell them. Rumour has it that a major offensive is in motion. Roberts is mustering his forces from all corners of the country, and he is in Belmont to inspect the readiness of the Canadians.

As though to confirm this, Colonel Otter exchanges more than pleasantries with the man, although Will is too far away to pick up any of the conversation. The soldiers are cheering so loud, he doubts that even Mason and Hardy can discern any more of that conversation than he can from their closer vantage point.

Will is more interested in the thick-necked civilian who stepped off the train with them, anyway. Shorter perhaps than Lord Roberts and wearing a pair of wire-rimmed spectacles, he resembles a strange little gnome.

He is passing something out to the troops. Digging into a sack he brought with him and distributing its contents to anyone who reaches out. Curious, Will follows Mason's earlier lead and pushes his way toward the platform. The bag is almost empty when he arrives. The little man turns like a top, his large belly contained by the lone button on his vest.

"And you?" he asks Will above the din.

Ignorant, Will lifts his hand over the heads of the clustering soldiers and receives a clay pipe for his efforts. He flips it over in his hands as the dandy disappears down the siding in the direction of the generals.

"Oi. How'd you like that?" A British soldier next to Will smiles after their benefactor. "Rudyard Kipling, that was."

"Pardon," says Will, slightly stunned by the news.

"Rudyard Kipling. What wrote the *Jungle Book*, like."

‡

The night before their march to the Modder River, Will is alone in the latrines when he senses someone behind him. His fly is unbuttoned and he is pissing into the open pit.

"Miss me?"

He recognizes the voice immediately as Kadinsky's. Will has run across him several times since Claire slapped him, but at no point was there any incident. It was as though he had receded like a whipped puppy, chastened and subdued. But now his voice is an iceberg, cold and edgy, concealing something ominous underneath.

Will is only too aware of his own vulnerability.

However, the man walks past him and steps up to the next stall. For a moment, Will relaxes, thinking that perhaps his presence here is only a coincidence.

The sound of the other man's urine hitting the soup beneath them resonates in the enclosed space.

"Do you know what happens to boys like you in prison?"

Suddenly, it dawns on Will that they are not alone. Calmly he buttons his pants. His heart hammers against the cage of his chest. Before he can turn away, his arms are seized and he is lifted off the ground. Helpless, he is spun to the floor. His face pressed close to the stinking earth. Will struggles against his captors, but one of them grinds a knee into the nape of his neck, making any movement excruciating.

Made still again, he listens as Kadinsky finishes his task.

"Tsk. Tsk. Don't make this any worse than it has to be." The man straddles Will's back, placing a big, heavy boot to either side. Then he crouches in close enough for Will to feel each puff of speech from his lips.

"Where are your nigger friends now? Your girlfriend?"

Will attempts to break free at the mention of Claire, but again the pressure of the man's knee cows him. He cries out, but not loudly.

"Don't flatter yourself, boy. I'm not interested in you that way."

Kadinsky runs his fingers through Will's hair and then yanks his head backward. He cannot help but whimper. His spine feels as though it might split.

Closer to his ear again, Kadinsky speaks, "I'm just here to tell you that it's not over. When you least expect it, I'll be there. I want you to live with that for a while."

When he lets go of Will's head, it lolls in the dirt, but the relief is instantaneous. He does not move as the men file out around him. The last gives him a kick for good measure. But not hard enough to do damage.

It is all he can do not to cry.

4

March to the Modder River

February 13 – February 18, 1900

*T*he mephitic funk of the rotting horse flesh reaches the troops before the borehole well is even in sight. Will is one of the first to stagger over the red crest of the kopje, waterless and parched. The thermometer at the rail line read one hundred and fourteen degrees Fahrenheit when they set out after breakfast. He has never experienced such devastating heat on the prairies. Not even the last few months of South African sun have prepared him. The air is an incandescent tide, and he is drowning in it. The soldiers are desperate to plunge into the well.

But wavering on the veldt beneath him are the charred and mutilated corpses of Kitchener's Light Horse. Ambushed by Boer marauders, no doubt, the day previous. Rearguard action that has characterized the enemy's stinging successes, but failed to slow the lumbering and relentless British march toward Kimberley. While the bodies of the more than fifty riders have been cleared from the reservoir, the mangled horses remain, arrayed haphazardly on the desert floor, attracting flies and pestilence.

Will trips down the hillside in the direction of the water, shoving the soldier in front of him, the soles of his own boots worn paper thin, the right one loose and flapping. The man falls forward onto his hands, sending a spray of stones down the slope ahead of him. But the sudden movement, awkward as it is, sets off a chain reaction in the line behind them. The soldiers break ranks, slipping and tumbling toward the open well hole. It is all Will can do to contain his own urge to run as he helps the soldier to his feet.

A British officer guarding the festering pond fires a single shot into the air above them, but even he cannot stem the flow of Canadian troops as they throw themselves at the pool. Stirred by the sudden rush of footfalls, the waters darken with silt. Oblivious to the perils of the water and the threat of the British officer, they slake their thirst with sand in cupped hands and gulping mouthfuls.

Even Will wades in after them, falling to his knees in the warm soup. He lifts the putrid stink of it to his mouth—slime-green strands of scum—and forces it down, swallowing hard. Immediately, acid rises in the back of his throat. Moments later, he trundles out to retch and heave among the dead horses.

When he is through gagging, Will wipes his mouth with the back of his sleeve and looks out over the veldt at the gutted Dutch homestead not one hundred yards distant, already the centre of a gathering brigade. Mules and horses corralled in among neatly piled stone knee-walls. A gaggle of spectators, dressed in khaki serge uniforms, eyes the confused arrival of the new men from Belmont.

Ramdam. This is the beginning.

‡

The sun is hot enough to melt teeth, thinks Campbell. He is drinking clandestinely from a wineskin full of Kaffir beer. His wife's greatest creation. Next to his children, of course.

"It's hot enough to melt teeth," he says.

"Jolly good, that one," says Barrett.

Campbell is afraid the man will pass out in the wagon again. He arrived in Ramdam a day before the Canadian troops were due and hasn't left the vicinity of Sophie's hut since.

"It's hot enough to cook puppies," says Barrett, smiling to himself.

"Puppies?"

"Yes. Can't stand them. 'Specially lap dogs."

They are playing a word game for lack of anything better to do. The children scurry around them. Barrett, if Campbell is to be honest, is poor competition, considering he is a writer by trade. The man's nose is a corpuscle. He is tempted to lance it.

"The lads," Barrett announces.

The balloonist recognizes the Royal Canadians flickering into view over the low hills surrounding the farmstead.

"Christ," he says as the soldiers stumble down the slopes toward the cesspool, doubling as a well. "Jesus Christ."

"It's hot enough to ..." says Barrett.

But Campbell is no longer listening. He has just seen an army of ghosts.

‡

Ramdam is a way station in the desert, south of the Riet River. The site of an armed conflict only days earlier. A farmhouse of blasted windows and ruined outbuildings. Yet, it is also the site of the largest massing of troops in modern history. More than fifty Canadians fell on the forced march the day before. Robert was brought in by wagon, along with the other fallen. Some with sunstroke. Others, like Robert, simply exhausted, dehydrated, and disheartened. Ramdam is only the first stage in their pursuit of Cronje. Will and his fellow soldiers are brigaded with the Gordons—or what remains of them, the Cornwalls, and the Shropshires. They have become the Fighting 19th. Combined with the 9th Division, also in the process of arriving, they number more than thirty-five thousand men, along with five thousand native drivers and more than twenty thousand mules, oxen, and horses. The artillery and supplies necessary to sustain the huge mob in a land of little vegetation require an additional seven hundred wagons and carts.

Will and Mason are lost in the sea of green and salt-caked khaki serge. Both men do their best to repair worn boots with rags tied about their toes. Will is forced to section off his green puttees with a knife to complete the job. Robert and Hardy are not better off. Wilson, of beetle-fighting fame, and Captain Blanchard are both pulled from the ranks for leg and foot injuries. A few others are sidelined with fever, the beginning of another enteric outbreak.

The Canadians, who came only with the packs on their backs, are without tents. Will rolls his greatcoat into a ball and uses it as a pillow. Mason and the others do the same.

"We should escort Robert to the medical unit," says Will as he faces his friend. Supper consisted of hard bread and canned meat—an unexpected delicacy—but not enough to sate his hunger.

"He's a grown man. If he can't do the march, let him turn himself in," answers Mason. The day's toils have managed to take the wind out of his sails. If only slightly.

"You know he won't do that."

"He won't thank you for doing it either. Besides, the medic isn't going to remove a man who's willing to march on. This isn't kindergarten."

Will decides not to pursue the matter further with Mason. He might even be right about Robert and the medical staff. The weight of sleep is on him in any case. And he knows that he must look after himself as well. His mind is full of foreboding. The troops gathering at Ramdam are grim with determination. Most of them battle-hardened already and looking for retribution. His own reluctance was never more apparent to him than it is now.

‡

The next day, they set out for the Riet River and Watervaal Drift. The 9th Division is to cross over. The Canadians and the Fighting 19th will traverse the waters the day after. No bridges exist in the desert, so the process is expected to be slow and arduous. The temperature is a few degrees cooler than the day before, but it makes little difference to the troops. Will feels the sun's punishment long before noon. His only consolation is that his boots seem to be holding after his makeshift repairs. Sweat darkens his uniform. He has not bathed since his brief stay in Douglas, and he has not changed his clothing since the regiment's posting in Green Point, months earlier in Cape Town. The stench of the men around him is redoubled by the faecal offerings of the livestock in their long drawn-out wagon train. If the Boer does not see the enormous dust cloud created by the British advance, they will surely smell them from their upwind approach.

He and Mason catch a lift on the back of a native supply wagon for several miles over flat ground. As the column snakes backward impossibly into distance, Will looks for Robert, but cannot spot him. The short break is a welcome relief, but once the troops begin to climb a pass to the west of a low kopje, the soldiers are forced to jump down and push. The obstinate mules offer little in the way of help. On the downward slope, Will and Mason abandon their places to Hardy and another private from A Company.

The advancing army reminds Will of a prehistoric beast crawling ignorant from its mud hovel onto land for the first time, where evolution will transform the slug-like, amorphous creature, give it legs and a terrible head that it will swing dumbly, sleepily, until awakened instinctively by threat. For as Will understands it, this single division, this outcast arm gathered from the sinew of nations around the world, is more than half the size of the entire Boer army spread thinly in commando units across an expansive state, sometimes in bands of no more than two or three hundred soldiers. Cronje, The Lion of the Transvaal, for all his wily courage, does not command more than three thousand men.

Already stung by Boer hornets, the beast is shaking off its slumber even now. Will is but a scale on its well-armoured back. As are Hardy and Robert. As is Mason, for all his dreams of bravura and glory.

‡

Robert abandons everything he knows. He is struck dumb by the sun. He imagines mirages everywhere he looks. His home on the western prairie growing from the earth like a geographic anomaly. A hoodoo resistant to wind and time. Veccha visits him with her arms full of books, and he tells her to throw them away. That they're full of lies.

When he can walk no further, he crawls. A soldier tries to give him a hand, but Robert sees only Veccha and shrugs the man off. The next time he looks up, the sun has turned black and floats only a short distance above the veldt. He tries to speak, but his tongue is too thick. His lips split with the effort.

A corpulent god steps from his chariot beneath the sun to gather him up. The smell of him causes Robert to gag.

"All right then," says the saviour. "You're worse than Barrett on an empty stomach. Up you go then."

Another pair of arms collects him, and together they drag him back to the wagons.

Campbell, thinks Robert. Oh, yes. We're at war.

‡

Water. Eventually his thoughts are reduced to this. Water and thirst. Time and again, the unrelenting South African sun strips away the layers of Will's complex mind, like the transparent skin of an onion. After twelve miles, most of it on foot, he is no different from the reptiles who scurry off at the sound of his approach, dreaming water, dreaming cool. That ancient part of his brain, the medulla, whispers to him. The animal impulse to drink suffuses all other thought.

When the Riet finally appears below him, its muddy chant is better than a wish. It has only been two days since they left the siding at Gras Pan, but they have covered a sizeable stretch of the Transvaal with little sleep and less water. Will cannot imagine the days ahead. Two or three more, perhaps. His mind cannot fathom the distance.

Like the men around him, Will wades into the shallows of the Riet, thankful for its caramel flow after the squalid stink of Ramdam. He is so parched that he could not cry if he chose to. Even the mounted infantry slip dazed from their saddles. Some, whose horses fell on the way, walk in on foot. Will can tell them apart by the knee-high boots. A terrible burden on the uneven ground between Ramdam and Watervaal Drift.

The 9th Division is already in the process of fording the river. Their oxen are mired on the far banks. Great naval guns lie silting in the drift. Several covered wagons are abandoned in the mud. A British major storms through the river, pacing furiously and shouting at the drivers. Will looks back at the tail of the beast. Campbell's great balloon bobs its way toward the river. Mason is nearby, but Hardy has disappeared. Will surmises he has fallen back like Robert.

Another officer joins the major midway across the river. Although their discussion is loud and animated, Will cannot make it out over the splashing of soldiers and livestock. The major abandons his efforts with the gun and marches back toward Will and the south shore. He grabs a corporal by the collar and hauls him up from where the soldier pries at a bogged wheel. After a brief exchange, the man nods and starts off at a run. Two more officers join the impromptu conference. One of those is Captain Arnold from Will's company.

"What's this?" Mason is dripping wet.

"I can't tell. Something's wrong." Will wades in the direction of the officers. Mason trundles alongside.

"Aren't we stopping here?" Mason asks no one in particular.

The officers march off as a unit before either Will or Mason arrive. "Campbell's here," says Mason. "Let's get it from him."

Will notes that the dark balloon is no more than a few hundred yards off, and nods to Mason. Either way, he'll be glad to hear the man's conversation. And his wife's purple ale would be more than welcome.

‡

Campbell watches the two soldiers approach like a couple of drowned rats. He is mildly drunk by his own estimation. The half-empty wineskin lies on the wooden bench beside him. Trailing those naval guns is an awful decision, he thinks. It will take a regiment to pull them over the banks.

Campbell belches, and lifts his hand in mock salute as Will and Mason draw near.

"You look like a Raja up there," says Mason over the din of the milling soldiers.

Campbell guffaws. "You must be mistaken," he says, indicating his crotch. "This is no trunk."

Mason swings himself up onto the wagon step, smiling. The column has all but halted in a bottleneck formation, awaiting its orders.

"I told you those guns were useless." Campbell waves dismissively in the direction of the fifteen-pounders. "You see, boys, it's not the size that matters after all. There's hope for you yet."

Will looks exhausted, Campbell remarks. His body has fallen in on itself. Shoulders slung forward, head low. Will tilts his face upward to address him, rather than lifting his chin. A company of Scots traipse past in search of the river.

"What do you think? We gonna get some rest here?"

Campbell takes a drink from the wineskin, offers it to Mason. He draws his left arm over his mouth. The dust tastes like iron.

"Not while those cannons plug up the river," he says. Mason passes the skin back, but Campbell shakes his head and points to Will, who could use it. The lad takes a long pull that ends in a fit of coughing.

"You're looking as bad as your man Robert," he says. It is not meant as a joke, though Will smiles weakly.

Once he has recovered, Will asks, "You know where he is?"

"A few wagons back. Or at least he was. Picked him up with four or five others from your outfit. He'll probably bring up the rear with those supply carts tomorrow."

A corporal from A Company arrives in search of Will and Mason. He is wet from the waist down. His sleeves are rolled past the elbow. "Otter says we gotta go haul them guns, boys."

Mason curses and then jumps down. Will passes the pouch back to Campbell.

"No rest for the wicked." The balloonist winks at Will, who offers a lopsided grin. Campbell watches them melt into the crowd as they move off toward the river, and then he squeezes the bulk of his body out of the wagon. He intends to find Siphokazi and to get the wineskin refilled.

‡

The Canadians are divided into teams of two hundred men. Each team is assigned one of the naval guns. The sun is long past its zenith, but that offers little relief to the soldiers. The fifteen-pounders are already harnessed to thirty-two oxen—an impressive force, but useless in the mud banks of the Riet. Some of the animals are buried to the belly and lowing pitifully. Will and Mason are side by side on the crest of the far bank. At least fifty other soldiers stand with them. A cord of anchor rope rests loosely in their hands. A similar squad mills further down the bank. Between them, and below, is the gun. Perhaps another thirty or forty men are scattered around it and the oxen, awaiting the order to push.

When it comes, simultaneously with the order to pull, Will and the others on his rope jump into action, pulling hard. The great gun rolls forward, its rivetted iron wheels creaking. The oxen cry and push into their britchens. A moment later, the rope begins to slip through Will's hands as the gun slides backwards, away from them. Others behind him fall forward. Beneath them, soldiers become mired in the silt and mud. The cannon rolls backward.

Will ends up beneath Mason, who topples under the pressure of the men behind him.

"Hand over hand," yells one of the privates from Will's company. Donald, he thinks. Or Doncaster.

A British officer peers through narrowed eyes. "What's that, soldier?" Clearly, it is not meant as an invitation to repeat the idea, but the private does not catch the subtle nuance, or else he chooses to ignore it.

"Hand over hand. Pull it in stages. You know," he continues, "one step at a time."

"Yeah," add a few of the men next to him. "We'll never do her all at once," says one.

The officer, flustered by their colonial insolence, turns and hesitates. Will imagines that his cheeks flush red.

But he gathers himself and stands and issues the directive nonetheless, calling down to those below.

Will sets his feet. This time, when the order comes, he draws the rope hand over hand and takes a single step backward. The line holds.

"Heave!" shouts Donald, again superseding the Brit. But everyone, to a man, heaves to. And then it becomes a chant among the men.

Will feels the strength return to his arms. His back ceases to ache, and he joins the chorus as they march slowly backward, dragging the cannon up the slope.

Water drips from the carriage as it lifts from the river. A cheer rises from the British forces across the drift. Will loses sight of the gun as the line proceeds back toward the open veldt, but he can see to his right, on the periphery, that another team has followed their lead. A second cheer goes up.

When the long nose of the naval gun tips forward and finally rights itself on flat ground, a soldier yells, "Let's take her all the way to Bloemfontein."

The Canadians join the ruckus on the far shore. Even Will breaks a smile and shares it with Mason.

Veccha,

If ever these letters find their way to you, I hope you will for-give me. I thought I was wrong to have married you. I know you felt it too, eventually. Mistakes are difficult to own up to, especially when you live in a world of absolutes.

But you are the reason for my transformation. Even though it has come so close to the end, I am glad to have had it at all. Most of us live out our lives otherwise. It is dangerous and frightening to have your faith shaken. To be suddenly without a net, and falling.

However, if you survive the fall, the process is liberating. I have no doubt that you will come to the same conclusions on your own. But I would like you to know that it has occurred to me as well. This might help you, afterwards. To know, I mean.

Love,
Robert

The next day's march is more like a stroll on the prairie, thinks Will. A breeze from the north rolls over the column and a flotilla of clouds does its best to block the harsh rays of the sun. He kicks his way through knee-high grasses, and in the distance, observes a line of trees—a sure sign of the river. The troops have orders to advance on Wegdraai Drift and set camp. A march of only half the distance covered the day before. Will's water bottle is full, and he has acquired a British flask as well. He slept on his greatcoat again last night, but he did not see Robert or Hardy. Both men remained with the supply wagons across the river, and will decamp later this morning. At times, the men strike up various songs from home, like "The Girl I left Behind Me," or a choice piece they've picked up. But for the most part, Will's march is quiet. He inquired the night before about the position of the field hospital, and was told there was a small village south of the Modder River called Jacobsdal that the 7th Division intended to take. The medical staff are travelling with that column. If the 7th does not receive any resistance, the hospital will set up operations in that hamlet.

It was reported that General French overran the Boer in Kimberley and is now pursuing a small force across the Transvaal to the north. The 19th is charged with stopping Cronje before he is able to ford the Modder and join that force. This means that the 19th must proceed through Jacobsdal if it is to have any chance of catching the Boer.

Cronje, as Will understands, can cross the Modder in only one of four locations. Klip Drift is the closest. Followed by Paardeberg Drift. Poplar Grove and Koedoesrand are further and, therefore, less likely targets for a Boer force hoping to outrun the British.

Upon their arrival at Wegdraai Drift, once again on the far shore of the Riet, Will's company is ordered to set a screen and cover the column as it crawls slowly forward. Kopjes to the southeast hold the menacing possibility of Boer raiders. All morning, Will leans over his rifle watching the blue hills and intermittently the 19th as it arrives in an unending stream of dust and noise.

It isn't until noon under overcast skies that anything eventful occurs. Mason, who had been sent for news by Captain Arnold, returns out of breath and slides down beside Will, who is prostrate behind ground cover.

"Something's up," he says in a whisper, although Will cannot see any reason for Mason to keep his voice low. "Two riders from the mounted infantry just came in. The officers are in a flurry."

"What's happening?" Will sits to receive the news.

"I think the Boer have struck at Wegdraai. Roberts is readying Kitchener's Horse and an artillery battery."

Will's mind, clouded by the news—weighing its importance—suddenly zeros in. "Are Robert and Hardy still there?"

Mason blinks. "I don't know."

"Ah, the best-laid plans of mice and men ... huh, boys?" Campbell is standing over them with his fingers in his suspenders, great hairy belly protruding from under his dirty shirt.

Will scrambles to his feet. "You know anything about it?"

Campbell's attitude changes. "One of the supply trains has been ambushed." He jerks a thumb backward over his shoulder. "Christian DeWet's boys. Maybe a thousand. Maybe less. On horseback, of course."

"Where did they come from?" Mason's eyes are dark, angry that he is not there, no doubt, thinks Will.

"North of the Orange River. Who knows?"

"A thousand men. Are they mad?" Mason scans the host buckling at the Riet River. Still arriving. Still winding backward to the horizon.

"Far from it. Lions look for the weak and the sick when they beset a herd of animals," says Campbell. "Isolate them and attack. Lord Roberts has neglected to assign the convoy with a guard. Colonel Ridley's got the only company in that region. Detailed at the drift."

"Will we have to turn back?" Will's expectations of meeting Claire are doused with the thought. But he thinks mainly of Robert and Hardy.

"Oh, we'll send relief. Some artillery. But my guess is we'll ultimately pull across the Riet. Leave the wagons there."

"Retreat?!" shouts Mason.

"Roberts has his eye on Cronje. The public needs a victory. He can't allow Smith-Dorrien and the 19th to get bogged down in a pissing match over food."

"What about Robert?" asks Will. "Have you seen him?"

"The column's still arriving," he answers. "He could be in any one of those wagons."

Will watches the slow drive along the Riet. The dark progress of the beast.

‡

At the hospital in Jacobsdal, Claire stares out the cracked panes of the low window leading out onto the dirt courtyard. She has just pumped morphine into the arm of a British soldier who is missing an eye. On the inside, the little Dutch farmhouse is comfortable enough. There is even a carpet upon which the patients can lie. One of the only valuable items not looted the day before. But outside is a different story. Soldiers sit, or stand, or pace in various degrees of undress. The walking wounded, Command calls them. Many of them have an arm tied in a white sling. A knee wrapped. Some are worse off, laid out in the dirt, close to the blue stone wall. Bodies leaking fluids through cotton presses. Kit bags are strewn about. A watering can stands absurdly untouched on the fence. Claire tries to imagine the woman who placed it there. A portion of the farmhouse roof and a wall have crumbled into one corner of the yard. A red-grey pile of stone, mortar, and tile. Those men who are able cling to the shade of a mangled thorn tree that grows against all odds in the dusty quadrangle. It is queer, she thinks, that no matter what their state of health, no matter what the outdoor temperature, all of them sport their gob helmets. Not one of them has bothered to remove it for the sake of comfort.

In all, the wounds are not many, given the sharp flurry of fighting when they first arrived. The Boer stayed only long enough to put on a show, and then departed promptly. Doctor Walpott has informed the nursing body to brace itself for an offensive in the days ahead.

"The tide is turning," he said solemnly this morning. He is a tall, gangly man of about fifty, with a great handlebar moustache. His hands, she has noticed at the operating table, are enormous. Yet this does not seem to impede his efficiency. He treats her well, which is more than she can say for her fellow nurses, who feel as Brits that they are clearly superior to an Aussie colonial.

But it is of no great consequence. She has Hilde. And according to reports from Cape Town, another nine nurses have arrived from Victoria. The first official contingent of Australian nurses.

Claire passes the bloke with a neck wound, just patched this morning. He has begged her for water throughout the night. A request she cannot fulfill. The results would be disastrous. Jacobsdal has not yet offered her anything comparable to the horror of Belmont in the week following Magersfontein. But her last weeks before decamping were spent nursing sunstroke and fever. This new influx of shrapnel and bullet victims is harder to deal with. She is satisfied, however, not to be steeled against emotion like some of the other medical staff. Miss Plimpton, the head-nurse from London, handles triage as she might shopping for cuts of meat.

"No, not this one. He's in God's hands now."

"We'll take this one at the elbow."

Claire smiles in spite of herself and immediately feels ashamed. She does not wish to trivialize the horror, but humour is sometimes all she has between herself and tears.

When she hears the sporadic cheers lifting through the yard, Claire is reminded that the Fighting 19th is due to pass through. Hilde walks briskly through the ward to the front door.

"Your beau, I presume," she shoots.

Claire gives her the evil eye, but Hilde only grins before disappearing through the portico. Claire has created a mess for herself, of course. She should hardly be flirting with boys at her age. But in some ways, she has never left her schoolgirl self behind. The problem is that

Will, she suspects, never was a schoolboy. Some people are born into adulthood.

And his silence is too much for her. She can't imagine what came over her that night on the road, or the afternoon she kissed him. Was it Mason's unconscious rejection? A claim on second prize? Or just another example of her own incautious behaviour? Even at the age of twenty-six, she is scolded for it. Her father blames her presence in South Africa on it.

She feels a bit like Pandora now. Waiting for hope to spring from the box she's opened.

‡

Robert and Hardy were on one of the last wagons to arrive. They missed all the action, according to Mason, who was hoping for Hardy's version of events. After a day and night of rest, they are back on the march—a short one—to Jacobsdal.

"So how did you know we'd abandon the wagons at Wegdraai?"

Campbell looks down at Will. The man's face is pinched as he stares into the bright rising sun. "What are you on about?"

"For a man with nothing but contempt for the British army, you seem to understand a lot about how it functions," says Will.

Campbell controls the reins over a team of eight oxen. "Haw!" he calls out to them.

"I don't mean to pry, or anything," says Will.

Campbell glances back at him, and then out over his team. Finally, he sighs. "Bugger it."

When Will looks up at him, he can see the man is smiling, but not happily. His mouth is a thin line tipped at one end.

"Some things never change, I guess."

"Sorry?"

"War, my boy. Once you've seen one, you've seen them all," Campbell adds. "Oh, sure. The body count will vary. The weapons will change. But there are always constants. Things you can depend on."

"So you've been in other wars?" Will is startled by the revelation.

"You could say that." Campbell takes a deep breath, "You ever heard of Khartoum?"

Will nods, and Campbell launches into a story.

"After the motherland lost interest in the Sudan, a General Gordon was ordered to organize a withdrawal of the country's Egyptian forces. I was a young man at the time. A few years older than you, but I'd been languishing a while in Egypt. My first real engagement didn't occur until Khartoum. I travelled south with Gordon in the Spring of 1884.

"Africa, you see, is an economic story to the Europeans. But to the Africans, it's a tribal tale. You can't begin to understand the delicate balance. A British withdrawal signals a free-for-all. Hens at a pecking match." Campbell glances down a moment, and then continues.

"The people of Khartoum welcomed us with open arms. We entered the city at the head of a parade. But leaving was a different story.

"A Beja uprising destroyed our lines of communication in the north, and before we knew it, we were isolated from Cairo in an increasingly hostile land. The Mahdists. The Ansar. The Beja. They all looked at us as a stepping stone to power in the vacuum we'd be leaving in our wake.

"I was sent out as part of a small offensive to clear the roads north, but the Egyptian officers betrayed us. We didn't fire more than a single salvo before the desertion began. We were forced to flee in the face of an insurmountable foe.

"When we returned, Gordon ordered us to dig in. And so we set about barricading the city, evacuating those foreign nationals that we were able. We planted mines which blew the Ansar at the moon. And we sent riders to Cairo. Begging for reinforcements. Which, we learned, were not to come.

"We became the weak calf. The herd had already moved on."

Campbell snaps the reins.

"Gordon's right-hand man was killed during an expedition in August. Like they had before, the Egyptian troops in his command scattered to the wind. Rats from a sinking ship. A flying column of camel troops attempted to reach us after an uproar in the British media, but they never made it through. Disappeared in the sands.

"We were like animals at a shrinking water pool. Literally. As the spring floods receded, the Ansar came knocking from the river. The siege was short-lived. They drove us back, building by building, until Gordon himself was beheaded on the steps of an old palace."

The balloonist pauses. Will can see his difficulty. The apple in his throat.

"I hung on with a small band of soldiers for two more days. The city was chaotic. Wolseley arrived with a flotilla of gunboats from Egypt, and tried to force his way into the heart of Khartoum. But he was outnumbered and outgunned. I managed to escape under a hail of gunfire that cut us to pieces.

"We arrived at the head of a parade, you understand. All that pomp and circumstance. But in the end, we were left to die by our own army. The cost of saving us was simply too high. We are the expendables, my boy. Flotsam on the tides of history. Driftwood."

‡

Hardy sends up a roar in response to the Brits and the Aussies who welcome them on the outskirts of Jacobsdal. Will suggests that Robert drop by the hospital for a physical, but the older man pretends not to hear. The Canadians, anticipating a rest stop, fan out among the ruined homes to forage with the troops already occupying the town.

Private Donald grabs at a chicken that streaks through the ranks. After stumbling and recovering, he manages to catch hold of its neck.

The squawking, quaking mess of feathers beats its wings in a bid to escape, calling much attention to the scene.

Campbell laughs, and Will stops to witness the comedy unfold. Mason and Robert and Hardy are also on hand. A circle of observers gawks. Donald, covered now in a spray of chicken shit, holds the captive bird aloft. His triumphant smile reveals a breech of crooked teeth. Several other soldiers laugh and spur him on. But Will is determined to seek out Claire, now that the column has arrived.

He nods to Campbell, but as he leaves the company, a chorus of boos erupts behind him. Will spins to find the British lieutenant who led them in the transportation of yesterday's cannon. He is only yards from Donald, who stares back and forth between the officer and the crowd, incredulous. The bird is suspended upside down like a collapsed parasol. It has calmed somewhat as though understanding its impending salvation.

"Arrest this man!" barks the officer at two nearby privates, face flushed as before under the stream of abuse from the soldiers. "You two, restrain him," he tries again.

"For what, sir?" asks the Tommy in question.

"Looting, of course. Now restrain this man immediately. That's an order."

The two British regulars step forward, averting the crowd's gaze. Everything has grown suddenly quiet.

"The rest of you stand warned," he says, looking quickly across the blur of faces. But his voice breaks in mid-sentence. No one laughs as he backs off in the direction of a low building surrounded by a posted guard. The privates follow with Donald in hand. He does not release the chicken.

‡

When she raises her head to find Will in the room, Claire fails to suppress a quick intake of breath. Nurses and wounded men walk around him as a river slips around rock. She had been changing the dressing on her throat injury victim and did not see him enter.

At least he is smiling, she thinks. And thank God, he has removed that helmet.

Otherwise, he looks terrible.

"I thought I might see you here," she says, because she doesn't want to hold anything else out to him. Not while she's still confused.

Will's uniform is little more than rags. The boots look ridiculous. She can tell that he stopped by the well to wash before entering. Dirt is smeared over his face. A dark line remains on the bridge of his nose, and he is tanned a deep red brown.

"You look quite the adventurer," she tries. Moving closer, she can smell the sweat, days old and ripe.

"We're just passing through," he manages as his first words.

"Not here for the night, at least?" Claire is not sure whether this is a relief or a regret.

"I'm afraid not. General French is making a run to close Klip Drift. We're going to march straight through."

"In the dark?" Claire feels more secure discussing the absurdity of military manoeuvres. Details keep them away from anything too personal.

"Yeah, it looks like Mason might finally get his wish." The mention of his name causes a bubble in her chest. She blushes.

"We'll be expected to stop Cronje at Paardeberg Drift, it seems." Will plays with the helmet in his hands, looks around the room. He turns the helmet over and over and then finally puts it on. "Just thought I'd say hi."

Hilde enters behind Will and rolls her eyes immediately. When Claire glares at her, Will turns to follow her gaze. In that brief instant, she decides to kiss him. She doesn't have the time to consider the consequences, and she is sure to regret it immediately, but she has always run with her intuition.

Claire takes an awkward step over the boots of the patient

between them. Her little manoeuvre ends up looking more like a skip in a game of hopscotch, and she catches Will's shoulders with her outstretched hands. He wheels to face her. It must look like she's attacking him, thinks Claire, just before their lips meet.

Hilde be damned.

‡

Campbell leafs through an article Barrett handed him days ago. It is the first indication that the correspondent has done anything but drink his way through the desert. But he is much better at drinking, thinks the balloonist, as he examines the flowery script.

"This is shit," he says aloud. His eldest son is asleep on the bench beside him. The others help their mother in the hut. Already a line has formed. Soldiers from all units hoping to supplement their meagre regimental meals.

He lays a hand on the boy's head.

The article is full of patriotic elephant droppings. Exactly what he's come to expect from the papers. Full of tripe about Mother England. Brave lads. Pip, pip. Cheerio. As phony as the author himself.

"Should have been an officer," says Campbell.

This time the boy stirs at the sound of his father's voice. His eyes flutter, turn up to the big man's face.

"Shh. Go back to sleep," he says, patting his son's shoulder. Smoothing his ragged shirt. "It'll be a long night."

Campbell considers the article in his hand, and then carefully extracts a package of matches from his shirt pocket, trying not to disturb the boy further. He strikes one and the sulphur burn fills his nose. Without hesitating, he holds it to the sheaves of paper. The bottom corner turns black and ignites. Slowly the flame consumes it, and Campbell flicks the last of it over the edge of his wagon to protect his fingers. It flits like a moth, and then disappears into ash.

‡

"What were you doing in there?!" says Hilde as she approaches the shade tree where Claire stands smoking. The little nurse's face is pinched like a dried raisin. The content and tone of her question harkens back to Claire's mother the morning Claire announced her intention to follow the troops to South Africa.

Claire blows a steady stream of smoke through her lips. "Oh, shut up."

Hilde looks as though someone punched her in the stomach. She deflates like a bellows. And Claire wishes immediately that she had used the same line on her mom.

"I'm only trying to help." Hilde manages to regain her composure, hands firmly on her hips.

"Yeah. Well, you're not." Claire is not ready to let her friend off the hook just yet. She looks away, over the fence line and into the veldt where the 19th slogs a hard road north and east. The sun, low and behind her now, casts long shadows.

In spite of the fact that her mind is in a constant state of unrest, she is more than capable of appreciating the sheer size of this host as it wraps itself around the leeward slope of a massive kopje and across the desert well beyond her vision.

"When you took a fancy to that other one, I could understand. It was exciting. We were in Cape Town, thousands of miles from home. From our parents, God bless them. But that was dinner and a show. A stolen kiss. Well ... it was like being in some novel, where all the men are brave and dashing." A silence falls between them as Hilde pauses for breath.

Claire hears the sound of the woman's hands slap against her thighs. Grudgingly, she looks back at her friend.

It's growing darker quickly. Hilde is pale as a laundered sheet. Dark blood stains her apron like patches of rust. The cap on her head is crooked, and the mess of auburn curls spindles out from under it. She has never looked so lovely, or so vulnerable.

"And the chance of finding him again in Belmont … well, I was tickled. I couldn't wait to read the next page." Hilde takes a step forward. "But I don't understand what's between you and Will. I don't think you understand. Your little romance isn't fun, Claire. It's like watching a funeral procession. I won't believe that you love him. And damn it, we didn't come here to fall in love."

Claire extends her hand, and Hilde grasps it with both of hers. "I'm sorry."

"Our job is in there," Hilde says, tilting her head toward the blasted wall. "With the wounded."

Claire tramps on the cigarette she's been smoking and adds her other hand to Hilde's.

"But what if there are other wounds?" It is a silly thing to say, though she doesn't mean it to be.

"You can't fix those," says Hilde, her voice turning sharp again. "And besides," she tries more softly, "what you're doing is like giving water to that fellow with the neck wound. You're only making it worse."

The light around them has all but disappeared.

"Do you think so?"

Hilde does not answer.

‡

"Are you afraid to die?" Will cannot see Robert's face, even though it is no more than an arm's length from where he walks. As such, he cannot gauge the man's reaction. Perhaps, subconsciously, this is why he chooses this moment to ask. He has elected to march alongside Robert even if the man falls out completely. Will cannot really justify this decision. He does it only because it occurs to him to do so. He certainly did not plan on discussing the meaning of life, though in retrospect, Robert's silence encourages such thoughts.

Will's question is greeted with more of the same, at first. But he has learned to let the silence sit for a while. Robert is a man who weighs his words carefully.

"I used to think that the earth was one large museum," he says finally. "That it was a wondrous display housed in a large glass case, and that I could peer into it and learn everything there was to know."

They march on again with nothing said between them, yet somehow Will knows that Robert is far from finished. They have travelled miles already, but tonight, there is time to let the man unfold at his own pace.

"I believed it even as late as Cape Town, though I had been shaken at least a year earlier."

"By your wife?" Will holds his breath once the question is loose, but Robert picks up the thread without hesitation.

"There are more things in heaven and earth, Horatio ..."

Will does not speak.

"It is difficult to admit that everything you have placed your faith in might be wrong."

Although Will turns his head to hear the man beside him, Robert, he suspects, looks only ahead.

"The earth is not so static. It changes, always. Wind on a rock face will reduce the behemoth to dust, given time. A river will cut into the earth for years, and then one day dry up over night."

Suddenly, and without warning, Robert pushes Will out of line. He stumbles over a large stone, but rights himself. The column of men moves past them. And then Robert's face is so close to his own, Will can smell his stale breath. The canned meat from dinner.

"The moment you begin to think you know everything ... the moment you have traced the extent of the museum ... then you are dead. And you can live a long time like that." There is no anger in

Robert's voice. No hint of malice. In fact, if anything, thinks Will, he is excited by the discovery of his own words.

He expects Robert to continue, to spout off like an ancient oracle. It's what Will wants from him. But the man only sighs after a moment. The great parade marches past. Eventually, they rejoin the ranks and walk quietly into morning.

‡

Campbell awakens next to Sophie with a stiff cock. A piece of his anatomy that he has not seen in years without the aid of a mirror. Outside the cramped quarters of his wife's wagon, the camp is relatively still. They arrived at Klip Drift just before sunrise and the soldiers are doing their best to sleep. Campbell pats the broad hip of the woman next to him. Squeezes her small sharp breast. Then he remembers the children, curled into the nooks of the wagon like mice. He cannot recall the last time he and Sophie made love. Not since they joined this ridiculous parade, anyway. But perhaps that is a good thing, considering her impressive fertility. Campbell is not getting any younger.

He shifts the bulk of his white belly away from her back, reluctantly, and extricates himself from the blanket. Once outside the walls of their caravan, he lets out a prodigious fart, and stretches his arms skyward. Shirtless, he pulls the suspenders hanging at his sides up and over his shoulders. Today, he thinks, I shall shave.

As he readies the bowl of water from their meagre stores, he makes a mental note to refill the barrels from the Modder, which gurgles brown and quick at the edge of camp.

The first draw of the razor is like breaking kindling. And over the cracked surface of the mirror in his left hand, Campbell spots the pissant who arrested the Canadian soldier for looting yesterday. He is walking stiffly in the direction of the river. As he draws near, the little officer nods his greeting to Campbell. The look of disgust on his face is poorly disguised.

The balloonist waits until he is almost past before he spits a wad of phlegm at the man's feet. The officer pulls up, looks for witnesses.

"Morning, Lieutenant," Campbell says, readying the razor for another trial.

The man steps around the offending spot, and continues along his path.

After a few minutes, Campbell winks at his fresh complexion in the mirror. "You are one handsome devil," he addresses his reflection—a mug that widens into a look of surprise as a hand closes around his crotch. He turns to discover his wife.

"Hmph," he grunts. And she wipes a speck of soap from his cheek.

"Yes, you are," she says.

And Campbell feels himself stiffen again.

‡

Hardy tells them all the news just after mid-day. General French, who plugged the whole at Klip Drift a day earlier, finally caught up with Cronje at Vendutie Drift—a small ford upstream from Paardeberg.

"Caught them in the midst of breakfast," he says, assuming his characteristic storytelling stance. Knees bent, his body folded slightly at the waist and leaning forward. His meaty hands spread out in the air before him. "Some of the men were even napping on their saddles. The horses off grazing."

Mason throws a smile at Will, who is unsure whether the gesture is meant as a shared joke about Hardy's histrionics, or excitement at the prospect of impending battle.

"French sweeps in with twelve hundred cavalry, backed by two divisions of artillery," the corporal continues. "You can bet the smash of lyddite shells was enough to wake the burghers." Hardy shares a laugh with a few of the assembled privates.

"He chased them clear across the river," beams Hardy. "They're buried in a laager west of Paardeberg Drift."

Buried, thinks Will. Trenches. Another Magersfontein. But the others talk on.

Uncle John,

We're up against a river now. Sorry it has been so long since I've written. We've burned like a black powder fuse across the desert for days. The enemy is close and burrowing into the veldt. Mason says it will be like shooting prairie dogs, but I do not believe him.

The mute have begun to speak. Only I'm afraid to listen. Sometimes we need a holocaust to wake the dead.

I saw Claire, by the way. It was two days after St. Valentine's.

Will

5

Paardeberg Drift

February 18 – February 27, 1900

atteries drop lyddite shells into the Boer wagon laager across the Modder. Their thunderclap rips open Will's chest. He is deaf after the first volley. Black boys run up and down the south bank delivering coffee and biscuits. Will is given a shot of rum. The clear burn of its heat awakens him. His hands shake. He has not slept. The entire division marched through the night. Twenty-three miles. Twelve hours.

Across the river, the Boer crouch in narrow slit trenches. The Modder roars over the drift in flood. Somehow, the Royal Engineers have fashioned a rope line across. A thin umbilical thread. Atop a hill on the other side, signalmen with mirrors and flags direct the British guns.

Captain Arnold and the company sergeant grip the men one by one and toss them forward, down the bank. The officer screams over the racket of artillery fire. His face inches from Will's. "Hold the rope. Regroup on the other side. Do you hear me?" He shakes Will once and then pushes him over the edge.

Will can feel the exploding shell fire in the earth beneath his feet. The constant pop and rumble leave him dizzy and unbalanced. He trips and scrambles over loose rock. The world tilts and suddenly he is on his back looking up at an impossibly bright sun. A fist gathers the material at his chest and hauls him up. It's Mason, pushing, shoving him forward toward the river.

Both of them slip in the mud, and end up seated in the shallows. Water moves over them. Will grabs the rope above his head to prevent himself from being carried away. Mason is already pulling himself up. Beneath the thunder is a new sound, like the amplified crackle of grease in a pan. Sporadic rifle fire. And even deeper, the slow moving chug of a Maxim gun.

As Will wades through the Modder, the rope is alive in his hands. It is yanked left and right, tugged up and down, as the men in front and back of him use it for balance.

The soldier in line before him turns and opens his mouth in terror, but no sound escapes. Will looks upriver. A chestnut horse hurtles toward them, uttering baleful screams. With the water up to his armpits now, Will cannot move. The animal streams past, taking the soldier with it. Another man is thrown loose and follows them.

Halfway across, Will pisses himself. A warm flood in his pants. When he reaches the other shore, his chest is heaving. He crawls forward and falls.

Mason yells, "Keep moving!"

Up over the bank, Will follows a line of men crouched and running to the right behind a rise of earth, toward a hillock in the distance. The troops have managed to ford one of the Canadian guns, which is rolled into place behind poor cover. It opens fire as Will passes beneath the ridge where it rocks with recoil. His skin jumps at the burst of noise.

Fanning out now, his company dances toward the advance firing line, where the Black Watch and the Seaforths lie prostrate, exchanging rifle fire with an invisible enemy, dug into the laager beyond. Will spies the blond-haired soldier from the football game. He is bent in an all-out run, his helmet lost, the rifle loose in his left hand. Will can almost trace the trajectory of the Mauser bullet that stops him. It slams into his chest, buckling his knees. A fine mist of blood suffuses the space before him like a cloud. And then he falls.

Boer snipers line a donga more than fifteen hundred yards away. Will dives to his stomach and crawls the rest of the way to the firing line, without once looking up. He experiences the next several hundred yards in flashes of lucidity, as though moments have been cut from his life. Finally, he reaches a tuft of vegetation—part of a scraggly treeline that originates in the flood plain of the river. Other men are scattered on either side of him, behind stone-hard ant hills and inside rock recesses.

A moment later, Mason is beside him, panting. Then Hardy and Captain Arnold. Robert stumbles in seconds afterward, crashing down on one side. Rifle fire explodes in the dust by his boot and, quickly, he pulls it under cover.

"Oh, my God. Oh, my God." Hardy, Will realizes, is hyperventilating. Rocking back and forth in a foetal position. His eyes are red with tears.

"Shut up, godamnit," screams Mason.

Robert reaches out and touches the corporal's shoulder.

The one-pound shell of a Pom Pom gun tears through the flesh of a tree just above Arnold's head. Splinters and pulp rain over him.

"Oh, my God," whimpers Hardy.

"I said, shut up."

"Fire into that stand of trees, along the river." Captain Arnold stares through a pair of binoculars at a stretch of vegetation nearly eight hundred yards away.

Will holds his rifle close to his chest. He lies on his back, taking deep breaths. Mason cracks off two shots and then ducks back under cover. Will exhales and rolls into place behind a rough edge of rock. A tree root snarls over it. He can hear the zip and whine of enemy fire spilling towards them, but the Boer snipers are using smokeless gunpowder, and he cannot fix their position. Bullets smash into the earth before him. One glances off the rock where he has set his rifle. He fires once, blind, and rolls back. His eyes meet Mason's.

Another one-pound shell splits a sapling next to them.

"Christ," Mason says between his teeth.

A third shell sings off the rock behind Will's shoulders, like the note from a musical triangle.

"We have to move forward," barks Arnold.

Hardy is crying quietly now.

"Give us the word," responds Mason.

And then Arnold's head snaps back. A Mauser bullet explodes through the top of his skull, showering Will with bits of blood and bone. Grey puddles of brain.

"Oh, Jesus!" he yells, but does not move. The officer's binoculars are shattered on the ground beside him.

"Fall back!" Hardy screams. He stumbles to his knees and turns to run. Mason grabs him at the waistband of his pants and pulls back.

"Lie down, damnit."

Will begins to shake seriously. He can feel the muscles in his forearms spasm. The rifle jumps. He closes his eyes, but it is as though he has lost control of his limbs. His legs stir in the dirt. His breath chokes him.

"Will!" shouts Mason. "Help me."

When he opens his eyes, Mason is stretched out on his belly facing the direction from which they came. He has both of Hardy's legs in a bear hug, and still the man claws his way back toward the drift. Will lunges forward, but Hardy manages to break Mason's grip and his boot catches Will under the chin as he falls forward. Hardy makes it ten yards before he is cut down. Two bullets. Through and through.

All around them soldiers are digging in. The dead lie mangled, and above the relentless artillery—the snap of Mauser bullets, and the pop of Pom Pom shells—there is the inhuman wail of the wounded like the cries of abandoned children.

Behind them, Robert is propped up in firing position. His rifle peeping in between brambles. Will and Mason slither back on their stomachs, but Will realizes what has occurred before they pull up alongside the man. He is too still. Slower to understand, but suddenly aware, Mason grabs the bigger soldier at the shoulder and turns him over in one fluid movement. The young man's eyes dart over the body. Robert's abdomen seeps blood warm and dark under pale desert serge.

"How?" Mason almost screams.

Will knows. "As he came in."

"But ..." Mason trails off.

Will thinks of Robert's soft words to Hardy, as the corporal cried like a child. His own stoic acceptance. His silence.

For the first time since he reached the river, Will can see beyond the moment. The man's death settles in. And Will is alive.

‡

The two of them bake under a knuckle of sun until lunch time comes and goes. And now they shiver beneath an unexpected cloud burst. Cold rain in fat drops. Sheets of it falling in waves. The Boer adopt a slow fire, husbanding their ammunition while under siege, for they know not how long. Will and Mason take turns firing into the treeline, but otherwise they do not talk.

They have outflanked Cronje. This much, at least, is clear, but they have accomplished little else. The enemy is too well hidden. Too well armed. Their sharpshooters make a game of the British forces within fifteen hundred yards.

Eventually, Will drifts off to sleep. His stomach is clenched tight as a fist. His throat dry. But exhaustion quells all this. During those brief moments, he sees Robert wading hip deep in the Canadian prairie before a rock wall that rises from the switchgrass to the height of ten men. Stretching out on either side as far as he can see. The structure breathes like a lung. Red ochre hunters chase abstract bison. Shield warriors do ancient battle. And slowly, Robert becomes them.

‡

Miles from the front, Claire listens to the ruckus of guns and thinks about the storms of her childhood. She is escaping. Allowing herself this.

She lived in a sprawling bungalow. Her parents still do. The earth was flat for miles around, and peppered with orchards. Little fruit-bearing trees like a cripple's hands. She could see forever. Predict weather long before it arrived. Hear it rolling in. Loved the tumult of a bruised sky boiling.

Electrical storms were her favourite. Curled into a porch swing with her dog—a wire-haired wolfhound the family called Spectre—she would watch them crackle silently on the horizon, igniting her senses one at a time. As they swept closer on a buffet of wind, she would feel their force on her exposed face. Her neck and hands. Then she would hear it burst like a cleared throat. A tubercular cough.

Rain was an anomaly in Albury, but when it came, she would race into the yard to embrace it. Once, her father caught her in the act and tackled her. Claire stared at him with crazed wide eyes. But as though to clarify his intentions, a bolt of lightning ripped a jagged crease in the sky—pulverizing a crooked plum tree at the edge of their field. It burned and burned in spite of the rain. By morning, it was a charred stump.

Who will be there to tackle Will? she wonders, as the artillery grumbles from the river.

‡

The touch of Mason's hand brings Will back to the world. The battlefield spins toward him as he surfaces from a dream he will never remember. Mason's face looms angular and absolute. The sun is low behind them.

"Aldworth is arriving with several regiments of Cornwalls."

Mason's hand remains fixed on Will's shoulder. His dark eyes penetrate. "Will. We're going to attack."

He cannot tell if his friend's intensity derives from fear or excitement. Perhaps these two emotions are inseparable.

"Fix your bayonet."

Will reaches across to touch Mason's shoulder in return. They have been friends since early childhood. Yet somehow they have lost each other on this voyage. Perhaps circumstances would have been different if Will had moved to Winnipeg. To university. He cannot know. But he hopes Mason understands everything he wants to communicate with this gesture. Today, it is suddenly important.

A moment later, he is preparing to do the unthinkable. Hands he once thought would be sullied in ink, wrapped around a pen, and used to tally figures in neat rows, are wrapped instead about the base of a steel bayonet. An instrument he hopes to drive into obstinate Boer farmers, who hide only a stone's throw from where he sits.

The first bugle splits the sky to Will's right, several others join in from all points. Will scrambles to his feet and clears the ridge of his safe haven. Out on the veldt, he screams until his throat hurts.

The Boer trench materializes in the earth before him and then erupts. Crossfire from the dongas is renewed. Will weaves his way around brambles and stone. Steps over the bodies of two Canadians, and passes one of the Cornwalls who has taken a knee and is in the process of falling. Two paces beyond him, Will trips over the sole of his own boot and plunges into the red dust. This is the only reason he is spared. The battalion collapses like a house of cards.

Will remains in the sand with his hands folded over his head until dark. Men moan and cry all over the battlefield. The gunfire turns sporadic, and then dies. He is still three hundred yards from the nearest Boer trench.

‡

Campbell is a mile behind the lines watching the traumatized troops creep in after nightfall. In a field west of him, a stand of wooden crosses litters the landscape—the remnants of a Scottish regiment. A handful of medical staff performs triage under a field tent. Stretcher bearers arrive and depart. Early estimates set the British casualties in excess of a thousand.

His balloon, which was grounded early on during the rainstorm, sits idle. He is dumbfounded by the order to charge. Even his brief assessment at dawn painted the picture of an impregnable foe. Officers have been quick to point fingers of blame all evening. But whatever the case—whoever is at fault—the results remain the same.

He shared a flagon of Kaffir beer with Mackenzie Barrett just before supper hour, assuming the worst was over. But when word of the failed assault trickled back, Campbell was furious. Even more so at Barrett's ludicrous reaction. His drunken "tally ho"s and his feigned Anglophilic mannerisms.

Campbell could not have been more relieved when the newspaperman finally passed out beneath the wagon.

The moment Mason and Will appear on the edge of the camp, the balloonist feels a surge of hope. He lumbers toward them through the press of men.

"Two sorrier-looking soldiers I never did see!" he exclaims. Campbell perceives the false joviality in his own voice. He touches them both to reassure himself that they are truly safe. "Let's have a look at you," he says, eyeing them up and down. "No holes. That's promising. Rain's on the way," he says, touching his own elbow. "My joints never lie. And we can't allow for any leaks."

He is appalled at the sound of his own voice, but can't help but prattle on. "Where's Robert?" he demands, looking past their shoulders.

"We tried to find him ... in the dark," Will answers. "But ..."

"We'll make it right tomorrow," says Mason. "You wait and see. We'll chase them from their bloody ratholes."

Campbell is stunned into silence His chest deflates, and he feels suddenly old.

"Shut up."

The man's head snaps up. Will is facing down the other. Campbell can see his jaw working in the low lamplight from the medical tent behind him. The lad's left arm twitches.

"I'm just saying," Mason states. "Damnit, Will. When are you gonna wake up? For Robert's sake."

Mason is lying on the earth before Campbell has time to process the quick reflex of Will's arm. It is a good punch. Catches the dark one leaning in.

Mason raises himself to one arm, but Will is on him like a terrier. He overshoots his mark slightly and the men roll over the ground. A circle quickly forms in their wake, opening like an arena.

But Campbell has seen enough. He nabs each of them in a great fat hand. Snatching them both from the earth like chastened puppies. Will's chest heaves. There's a tear in his left eye. But the anger slips from him almost as quickly as it came.

Mason is wiping his mouth, the blood ringing his teeth. Campbell allows him to twist clear. After a few steps backward, he spins on his heel and disappears through the crowd, which gradually folds in upon itself. The show is over.

"It's all right, son," whispers Campbell to Will. But he feels like a terrible liar.

‡

The Modder River is plugged with the carcasses of dead animals. The iron reek of dried blood is everywhere. By noon, the horses and the mules and the oxen will be turning black in the heat. The engineers do their best to remove them, but their number is too great. A gift from the Boer, who dumped them during the night. It is clear that Cronje can no longer escape, even if he wants to.

Will has attached himself to Donald, who seems to have gotten off with a reprimand for the chicken.

"They could have shot me at dawn, you know," the big man tells him, eyes wide. "Over a chicken." Both men shake their heads.

A Company is being sent in with the Shropshires and the Gordons. Their orders are to establish a firing line one thousand yards from the Boer. Apply pressure. Will is conscious that Mason stands in the same queue waiting to cross the river, but he hasn't spoken to him since their fight the night before.

The company sergeant informs the troops that the engineers were able to cross over several more Maxims before dawn to act as cover fire. The operation already seems to be proceeding with greater organization. Will's left arm, however, has not stopped twitching. Otherwise, he is calm.

Lieutenant Blanchard has stepped into Captain Arnold's shoes and stands next to the sergeant. His face is gaunt and white. The sky, although partly cloudy, promises heat and increased humidity. A haze lies over the river.

Campbell was right, thinks Will. Hard rains on the way. He slips into the river behind Donald and works his way slowly across.

‡

From his perch in the balloon, Campbell has a bird's eye view of the arena. Cronje has not been idle through the night. He has stationed commandos up and down the river in natural dongas. There are sharpshooters in the trees. Along the north shore of the river sits Cronje's laager, at the bottom of a shallow bowl. It is ringed by natural hills extending along the river west of Paardeberg Drift and bending slowly north. The laager is shaped like a sickle moon, but trenches have been dug on both sides of the river, making it a virtual fortress.

The air is thick, even at this height. Campbell wipes his brow with a filthy handkerchief and pockets the offensive cloth. In the far east, there are clouds poised on the horizon, but they will be long in coming, he thinks. No wind to speak of.

He thinks about the two Canadian soldiers as he observes the theatre taking shape beneath him. Their falling out. A long thin line of men wades into the river below. The distant rumble of naval guns tears open the dawn.

Will and Mason will be moving amid that line, unrecognizable and indistinguishable from Campbell's removed vantage point. As insignificant as bugs. Even the unprecedented buildup of troops is swallowed by the expanse of the Transvaal rolling away in every direction like a dirt green dome. The entire drama below is but a fly on the back of the African continent. And yet an entire empire holds its breath, awaiting the outcome.

‡

Donald and Will dig themselves shallow trenches and lay their heads in the sand. All day the Boer unleash the loathsome Pom Pom guns. The one-pound Maxim-Nordenfeldts. For the most part, the deadly shells sail clear over the advanced firing line, but their deadly song carves up the air. Only the most foolhardy attempt to return fire. The sun, more than the Boer artillery, doles out its usual punishment.

The British water carts are driven from the field each time they endeavour to reach the troops. Not even the stretcher bearers are safe. A Boer sharpshooter wreaks havoc from the trees. The Canadian Maxims have tried to cut him down all morning, but he remains there still. Out of range, perhaps. Will does not raise his head to find out.

His battle is waged against the fire ants instead. Stealing over the veldt from their impregnable towers, their red-jewelled bodies pester him relentlessly, biting into the exposed flesh of his hands, the back of his neck. And eventually, they infiltrate his uniform, terrorizing him from within. Though he swats and pinches the little beasts, Will dare not sit up or even raise his head. Before midday, he is covered in welts.

The whole operation is futile, if much less bloody than the debacle of the day before.

"Psst. Will." Donald calls to him from his dugout an arm's length away.

Will turns his head to the left, so he can see the man. "What?"

Donald is prostrate, with his ear to the ground. A mirror image of Will.

"You got any water? I'm done for if I don't get a drink." The soldier's face is caked in red dust. A nasty welt swells under his right eye. His lips are cracked.

Will's bottle is depleted as well, but the British flask he picked up is still half-full. Drinking from it has been an exercise in contortion. "Yeah. Gimme a minute."

Will, who is closer to the treeline, is worried about sharpshooters. Particularly the unreachable fellow in the branches.

"He's dead," says Donald, reading Will's mind.

"How do you know?"

"I can see him from here. Must have at least four hundred holes in him. The Maxims just keep firing."

"Then why doesn't he fall?"

Donald smiles, splitting his lips. "Tied to the tree by his belt."

Will fumbles with the small canteen and nudges it across the veldt between them. Donald reaches out. "I can't get at it. Give it another push."

Will stretches his arm along the ground. Fingers the metal flask. That's when the bullet strikes. It shatters a stone in an explosion of earth, and something lodges itself just back of Will's wrist. He screams in spite of himself.

"Jesus," says Donald.

Will rolls onto his back and clutches the damaged hand to his chest.

"Stop moving, for crissakes."

The bullet came from the direction of the trenches. If he sits up or even rolls again, he is likely to be shot a second time.

"Hang in there," Donald reassures him, though Will can barely hear his voice through the pain. "It'll be dark soon."

The twitching, at least, has stopped.

‡

The rain is coming in through the roof, gathering in the rafters, and falling in a steady drip by the altar. The hospital has expanded its operations. Claire is one of the nurses transferred to the small Dutch Reform Church after the wounded were shipped back from Paardeberg the day before.

Twenty Canadian bodies are buried in the yard. Sixty more populate the two wards. Will and Mason are not among them. That is what she holds onto.

One of her earliest patients was a Private McCreary. Head wound, the chart said simply. Head wound, she thinks. His brains had been stuffed back into his skull by another soldier. A stretcher bearer held them there with a bandage. He was, against all medical possibility, awake when he arrived, though he couldn't speak beyond a gurgle. She isn't sure if he could even understand what was happening to him. When she unwrapped the tape, his brain oozed onto the bed. He died watching her.

A Private Clarke was shot five times in the back and abdomen. It is likely he was used as a shield by his comrades, who took him for dead. He is in recovery now.

She has run the gamut of body parts since yesterday at dawn. Feet, shoulders, legs. Throat. Pierced lungs. Shattered faces. The boy in the bed before her—Private Shaw, A.C.—was shot in the groin and is likely to bleed to death before the day is out. She has not slept or eaten anything more than a biscuit since the eighteenth. Two days ago.

Her nerves are frayed. She's out of cigarettes. And this is how she discovers Will when he walks onto the ward.

"Hi," he says, carrying the veldt on his uniform like an armour. His face and hair are also caked with it. Only his forearm is clean to the elbow, where he's been sewn shut and bandaged.

She leads him by his good arm, past the wounded and the other nurses carrying out their treatments. Irrigating wounds. Changing dressings. One woman sleeps between a patient and the wall.

The yard is already dark when they free themselves from the close air of the church. They sprint through the rain in the direction of a white bungalow. The nurses' quarters.

She shares an attic room with Hilde. A half-storey with a small dormer window letting out onto a ruined garden.

She is aware that what she is doing is wrong. If they are caught it will be terrible for both of them. But not only that. She does not know the soldier at all really. He hasn't allowed her to know him. So what she intends has nothing to do with love. But she doesn't care. It's about need. Which is what passes for love here. And after everything she has seen in South Africa, that is more than enough. She will take what she can get. Small mercies.

‡

He sleeps the rest of that day and through the night. The following morning, he is able to take a short walk, but when the throbbing becomes too intense, Claire administers morphine. He slips in and out of a drugged haze of dreams for the rest of the second day, awaking finally in the hours before dawn.

Claire has been with him at points. And at other moments, he has awakened alone. But she is with him now, staring through small tired eyes. The room is lit only by the amber glow of a low-burning hurricane lamp.

He has not done this before. But he is certain that it is new to her as well. He hardens under her touch. Feels the same quickening he first experienced in the darkness of his childhood room above his uncle's store. It's a process of rediscovery. Her mouth meets his, and Will falls backward onto the bed. She crawls on top of him without hesitation, and a moment later she cries out. After only a slight pause, she begins to move again. Will closes his eyes, sheathed inside her. Works his hands up under her smock on either side of her rocking hips. But he is too late.

It happens so quickly. He stills Claire only in time for his orgasm to pass into her. When the spasms subside, he lies back, aware of the small room—its angled ceiling—as though for the first time.

Claire begins to move again, slowly, until she too shudders. Lips drawn tight. Eyes clenched. And then it is as though someone releases a spring within her. She gasps. Almost a weeping. And leans forward over his chest. The dirt of the veldt covering both of them now.

‡

The rains relent in the hours before dawn. The sky, through the tiny dormer window, is still fat and bruised with cloud. Will touches the wound on his left wrist, where there is a dull ache. Miraculously, he has full mobility of the hand.

"Stones," the doctor whistled. "Only but grazed the bone. Lodged in tight, though."

The gangly man was staring at a dark plate of glass. Holding it up to the light. An X-ray, he called it. A miracle of modern science. Will could trace the pale ghost of his skeletal self captured in the glass. The doctor offered it to him, and he had accepted. Wrapped it into his kit bag. Claire had been amazed by it. Although some of the nurses spoke about the magical camera, it was the first time she had seen its product with her own eyes. They had nothing like that in Canberra, she was sure of it.

Although they do not see much of each other that day, Claire brings them a meagre picnic of bread and canned meat late in the evening. She also brings up a bucket and a sponge so that she can wash him. He flushes under her gaze. Conscious of his own nakedness next to her.

They make love more slowly the second time, though somehow it seems just as urgent. This time she removes her dress. He does not have to ask her. It is as though she has read his mind. And he wants her then. The pale phosphorescent bowl of her belly. The dark triangular thatch beneath.

It is awkward and lovely. Far more so than the first time, when both of them were driven by something other than desire—fear maybe, or need. But once he is inside her, it is the same. Slightly melancholic with the promise of euphoria.

He is glad that it is Claire beneath him, because he knows that she understands everything he needs to lose. And there are those few seconds during his release when that will happen absolutely. But he suspects that it is different for her. That it is not about forgetting. It is about receiving and accepting. By offering him a chance to forget, she is saving herself. And he also suspects that it would not be the same with someone else. That possibly, it will never be the same between them afterward.

He knows that he will be returning to the front. If not in time for Paardeberg, then it will be Bloemfontein. And, if he survives, Pretoria. And then, perhaps, there will be a boat to take him home. He has to look ahead, because he is human and that is his destiny. But there is also the present to consider.

Outside, night has fallen again. Beside him, it is Claire's turn to sleep. Will turns from the window. He will need new boots, he thinks.

‡

Claire is suffused with wonder and energy as she bustles among the wounded. She has not spoken to Hilde about the last two nights, and yet she is sure her friend is aware of the change. It is both less and more than Claire imagined it to be. She abandoned the idea of modesty in Belmont. Ministering to the needs of dying men's bodies has stripped away most of the mystery. But as she lay in the dark pressed naked against Will, she understood that there were different mysteries she had yet to unfold.

The vague yearning Claire possessed days ago, she can only describe as adolescent. But afterward, touching Will beneath the sheets, she became aware of her own desire as something more acute and deliberate. A feeling she imagines men develop at an earlier age with the first stirring of their cocks.

As children, she and Hilde used to watch the stallion courting the mares at pasture and the two of them would giggle and blush at his obvious excitement. But now she understands the erratic behaviour of the mares.

Initially, she was only conscious of what she could offer Will. It was purely psychological. Now, she realizes that there is something she can take. Not love. But something physical and intuitive. And it anchors her in a place, where logic and reason no longer apply.

‡

The veldt has accepted Robert, along with the others. Will stands before the cross that marks his place. Soon, this too will be gone. Deserts are studies in erasure. If Will learned anything from the man, he should not feel sorrow. And perhaps he doesn't. But at least he is feeling again. Loss, perhaps—which is not quite the same as sorrow.

In the beginning, Will doubted the older man's sanity. But in the end, he understood that he was perhaps the only truly sane individual among them. He was not meant for war.

This morning, Will offered his assistance in the wards, moving bodies, fetching water. Here he met the French doctor, Fissette, a little wrinkled man with a full head of white hair standing on end. He spoke terrible English with a thick accent, and greeted each patient the same way—his speech peppered with obscenities.

"Damn, you are very bad this morning. Hell, what can I do for you?"

Afterwards he would sit at the edge of their beds, or crouch by their mats placed on the floor, rubbing his round head. Then he would jump up and bark unintelligible orders to the nurses on hand. If the wounded men were not frightened before his arrival, they were when he left.

Will would like to share this with Robert now. To let him know that he understands the absurdity of it all. Instead, he places a pebble at the foot of his cross—smooth and dark—before he turns and walks back toward the church.

‡

"South of Portage there is a river," he says. "The Assiniboine."

Claire lies on the bed propped up on one arm, watching him. He is sitting at the head, leaning back against the wall.

"We swim there in summertime. In a stream that branches off and flows parallel to the river. It's the site of an abandoned mill. A footbridge leads across to a stretch of land. An island, I guess. Though it doesn't look that way."

He has changed uniforms. Wears new boots and corduroy trousers. He has spread out a lunch of bread and cheese on a white sheet, outdone only by the bottle of Fisherman Pure Scotch Whiskey, the product of much haggling. Raindrops smash against the windowpane above his left shoulder.

"Anyway, someone tied a rope to the rusted mill works. No one knows who. It's always been there. The idea is to swing from a second-storey window and let go mid river. From below, it looks easy. But once you're standing in the vacant window it seems impossibly high. Just reaching for the rope is difficult."

Hilde has grudgingly vacated the room. The rain has halted the advance at Paardeberg Drift, and the hiatus is a blessing at the hospital. The worst cases have been transported to Enslin Siding by wagon and shipped south to Cape Town by rail. For five days, almost without break, it has rained. Claire knows it cannot last. She has dubbed their clandestine meal "The Last Supper." The wine has been substituted by a foul-smelling purple drink that Will was able to lay hands on at considerable expense. It is a poor replacement.

"The first few summers you go there, you watch the older kids, and you lie to your friends. 'I did it once,' you say. And of course, they know you're lying. But they ask you what it was like anyway. And so you tell them the way you imagine it."

Claire is so comfortable she could fall asleep to the gentle cadence of Will's voice. Until he mentions Mason.

"He always bragged about it," says Will. "And even though I had been with him each time, and knew there was no way ... I could almost believe that he had. His description was so convincing."

She knows about their recent fight. It does not surprise her when he mentions it. Hilde said they were like two stags.

"But eventually, around the age of ten or eleven, you get your chance. You become the big kids. And a river of little kids flows beneath you, bobbing and waiting and lying amongst themselves.

"I remember we were all there in the cool hollow of the loft. The sound of water. The quality of light in the open windows made you think you were staring into the future. We were nervous. All of us. Even Mason. We teased each other. Called each other names. Issued dares and double dares.

"But it was like I wasn't really there. I just kept staring at the rope outside the window, dividing my childhood in two. Before and after." Will demonstrates with his hands, palms up on either side. First one, then the other. "Mason was supposed to jump first. Everyone expected him to be the one. He was always the first. But then, something happened." Will stares at the wall behind Claire, as though he can see the rope. The open window, beckoning.

"Mason had described it in such detail that I felt like I'd been doing it forever. So I jumped. I ran right past them before they even knew what I was doing."

"And what was it like?" Claire asks.

"Like nothing I'd ever expected," he says. "Mason had it all wrong. Just like South Africa."

‡

The harlequin is uglier than he remembers it. Paint chips flake from the cherubic face. It glares through vacant eyes. The smile is red and garish in a sea of faded rose. The tiny checkered outfit is tattered and worn, and one of the porcelain feet is broken, leaving a jagged edge.

Will wraps the doll back up in the dingy cloth that has cradled it since Sunnyside. It is precious to him, nonetheless, because it survives. This is why he must give it to Claire. Scarred, but not ruined.

When she enters the garret room, Will stuffs it beneath the pillow on her bed. His cheeks burn.

Claire closes the door with an almost imperceptible click, turns, and leans back against it. Her apron is stained.

Will imagines the doll's discovery days after he is gone. It is a satisfying thought. He moves toward her because she waits for him. Rain falls all over Africa.

‡

The arrival of four five-inch Howitzers and additional men is enough for Campbell to deduce a renewed advance. Smith-Dorrien has been ordered to bring this to an end. The Empire needs a victory, he thinks.

Among the new arrivals at Paardeberg are the convalescents from Jacobsdal. And Will is one of them.

Campbell blocks the soldier's path with his considerable girth. "Found a new pair of boots, I see."

The young man is dressed in Boer trousers and a soft hat as well. "I guess the other fellow won't be needing them."

"I don't suppose he will. How is the arm?"

"Sore. But I can still carry a rifle." The irony in the soldier's voice is new, but not caustic, thinks Campbell.

"That will come in handy tonight," quips the balloonist.

"It's been decided, then?"

"Not officially." Campbell lays a finger at the side of his nose. "But tomorrow is Majuba Day, and revenge is a dish best served cold."

Will cocks his head to one side. Squints.

"Never mind, my boy. I'll tell you all about it shortly" says Campbell. "Someone's been missing you." He lays a paw on Will's shoulder and ushers him back to his wife's wagon.

"Sophie," he calls, when they are within range. "Two cups."

She shouts something back, and Campbell is happy the visitor cannot comprehend.

‡

When Will and Campbell draw up to the wagon, Mason and Barrett are playing chess. A white canvas sheet has been rigged up, providing shade now, although most likely it has been preventing rain most of the week.

They are using Robert's chess set, Will realizes.

"Your friend is entirely unschooled in the game," barks the newsman by way of a greeting. "Full of brash, ill-conceived rushes and last minute defences. Hopelessly dangerous," he adds. "The damn fool's beaten me three times running. I swear he's a Boer."

Campbell laughs, and Mason looks up. The frown of concentration does not leave his face.

"Welcome back, old boy," says Barrett. "I see you've been frolicking with our nurses."

Will nods, feeling heat rise to his face.

"Campbell thinks we'll be attacking tonight," says Mason, as though nothing has changed. When, clearly, everything has. "Some mumbo jumbo about Majuba Day."

"So I hear," says Will.

"Probably get a medal for that." Mason flicks his head and points to Will's arm. "You okay?"

"I say," interrupts Barrett. "What is this Majuba Day I keep hearing about?"

"Let me explain it over a drink," says Campbell.

"Jolly good idea, Scott."

"Like to stretch your legs at the same time?"

"Not in the least. But if you insist." Barrett struggles to his feet, and Will realizes that this is not his first cup of ale today. "I say, where in the devil can a man take a piss in private around here?"

And then Campbell leads him away.

Will spies Robert's kit bag and the letters he wrote in the open mouth of it. Without thinking, he bends and takes the stack of them. Crushes them amongst his own things.

"I'm beginning to like this game," says Mason, when the two friends are alone. "Have a seat, and let me thrash you at it."

Will gathers the soapstone figures in his hands, and remembers them taking form in Robert's, as he sets them on the board.

‡

184

The moon has not yet risen, and the veldt is dark as a closet. Will has advanced to the firing line, now within eight hundred yards of the Boer trenches. He is sandwiched between Mason on his left and the champion beetle wrestler, Wilson, on his right. Behind them, the Gordons are preparing to take up the Canadian positions once they are vacated. Somewhere in the dark, the Shropshires support the flank.

The order to advance is whispered up and down the line. And slowly the men stand. Will carries his rifle loosely in his left hand. The wound is numb. With his right, he clutches Wilson's sleeve. They are to advance this way as far as possible, and establish a new firing line. In the rear, the men carry spades. And even further back, a team of engineers transports pickaxes and empty canvas sacks.

The late moon is a necessary evil. It blankets their movements from the Boer, but it heightens the risk of sounding the alarm. Snapping an ill-placed twig. Kicking a stone. Will is astonished at their luck—and the stealth of which two hundred and forty men are capable. Twenty-five minutes pass, with the clandestine force moving in short twenty-yard bursts.

Will begins to fear they might have veered too far and be crossing in front of the Boer dugouts. Or worse, that they are on course and moments from stepping in one.

In the black, someone trips a line of empty meat cans. His curse is crisp and clear. Will is face down in the veldt before the first shot cracks open the air. And a moment later, a storm of lead streaks over his head. He can hear soldiers falling all around him.

The troops in the rear begin digging madly. The dull hack of their spades comes to Will under the louder bark of Mauser fire. Mason's rifle flashes beside him. Will points his own rifle in the direction of the Boer trenches and snaps off two shots as well. He fights the panic rising in his throat. Others are breaking ranks under the heavy barrage. It's obvious from the flash and wink of the Boer rifles that the Canadians are less than one hundred yards from the enemy trenches.

Will knows they cannot stay. When the moon rises, the Boer will pick them off one by one. But it's seven hundred yards back to their own lines. The odds are no better in that direction.

A Canadian soldier is screaming and sobbing somewhere not far from Will. "Oh, God. Oh, God!"

Mason scuttles forward, without warning, into the black. Will attempts to follow, but a rifle shell strikes the earth in front of him, spraying sand and small particles of stone into his face. Temporarily blinded, Will hugs the ground, fingers pressed into his eyes. The sensation is not one of pain exactly, but annoyance. He tries to blink.

Off in the direction of the screaming soldier, there is movement, the sound of heavy running footsteps, disappearing in the direction of the British lines. A second later the run is cut short. The soldier grunts in mid cry and is quiet.

Peering through tears, Will seeks out his rifle and inches his way forward. He is completely unaware of his position in relation to the other Canadian troops. While his left eye is clearing, his right remains choked with debris. Using his hands, Will searches for cover. He moves snake-like toward where he thinks the river should be, and before long a natural gully opens in front of him. It is shallow, but large enough to fit his entire body if he draws up his legs. It is perhaps a dried-out pool left over from the river's seasonal flooding.

Shivering in the chill night air, and foetal in his safe haven, Will attempts to clean his other eye. A lyddite shell erupts behind him, raining down further detritus and rubble. He swallows down his rising panic, only to be shocked seconds later by the full force of someone else's body—a running tackle from another soldier seeking shelter from the hail of rifle fire and mortar bursts.

Will is driven from the gully, winded and disoriented in an invisible cloud of dust. Pain, blunt and acute, radiates from his kidneys. He crawls back, shaken, to the hole, which is now occupied.

Squinting, he can just make out the familiar Canadian uniform an instant before something dull and heavy cracks open his cheek. His field of vision dissolves in a hot white flash.

A bullet, he thinks.

But when he reopens his eyes, Will knows this is not the case. It was the butt of a rifle.

Another shell bursts, further away this time, but still the earth shakes with its impact.

Lying on his side, Will tries to understand the ramifications of this new situation. His thoughts are slow and muddied by a ringing in his ears. He touches the space on his face where the skin has been opened, and his fingers come away sticky with blood.

He does not anticipate the arrival of a second blow, but when it comes, his hand, moments earlier against his torn cheek, bears the brunt of this fresh trauma.

Still tender from its recent wounding, the appendage sings with renewed anguish. Will cries out, and rolls away, cupping his shattered mitt with the other. His rifle is lost.

Amid the searing pain, he tries to focus. Boer gunfire zips through the air above him. He must return to cover.

Again, Will rolls, protecting his wounded hand, but this time toward the shallow sink from where he was forced. The inertia of this movement sends him up and over the other soldier. He can tell from the man's grunt that he was not expecting this tactic.

But Will cannot take advantage of his surprise, and almost immediately, he feels the end of the man's elbow in his nose. The snap is crisp. Too late, Will covers his face. He hears sobbing, only this time, he realizes that the sound is that of his own.

For a moment, he imagines Mason arriving just in time to stop the attack. It is a juvenile thought. Cowardly, even. But it is there. He wants to cry out, but his assailant is relentless. The man's hands are tight against his throat. Thumbs pushing against his windpipe.

There is not room enough for two men in the gully. It is a matter of survival for both. Ideas about brotherhood, or any other naive notion of war that Will managed to hold onto, is obliterated by this last simple principle. They are beetles battling in a can, he thinks.

Feebly, Will sticks his ruined fist into his attacker's face, while he pries at the vise-like grip of the man's fingers with his only good hand. He is dizzy with the lack of air.

Only when the soldier leans in close, pressing with all his strength, does Will see who it is. That it should be Kadinsky seems only fitting. It doesn't even surprise him.

Thoughts of Uuka, fevered but fighting, flit through Will's mind. Images of Claire kneeling by his plaited cot. His uncle John sweeping the store at the end of a long day. Campbell with his youngest son on his knee. Robert carving. Mason crossing the finish line.

Will touches the earth beside him, searching for his rifle. It is a desperate hope, and a fruitless one. But he does find a stone, smooth and warm, spit up from the river after years of silting. He turns it over in his hand, the heft of it almost too much for him now.

Kadinsky's face swims in and out of focus. Will has never wanted anything so much as he wants to live right now. So he swings the stone like a hammer, bringing it down solid behind the man's ear, where he feels the skull give way.

After a moment, the battle sounds return, and Will finds himself gasping and spitting—the weight of Kadinsky's dead body against his own. He shimmies out from under it, coughing and heaving. The rising moon is visible now above the horizon. The Boer rifle fire has grown sporadic.

They are waiting, thinks Will, for the full light of it to guide them.

Off to his right, he can see Wilson, oblivious to the struggle that occurred only a few yards away from him. He cannot rest, thinks Will. He must leave the safety he so dearly won and seek out the natural folds along the Modder River. It cannot be far. Will pulls himself over the burnt earth toward Wilson and reaches out to grab his jacket. He speaks only through the insistence of his gaze, and Wilson follows.

Together, they gather the few remaining men in their company as they pass behind them on their stomachs.

After several minutes of crawling, Wilson calls to the soldiers, who make their way toward the river. He's found the bank. They veer instinctively toward his voice. One by one the soldiers drop over the side. To Will's surprise, Mason is at the end of the line and the last one to find the ridge and drop over. Will is dragging him by the hand when he cries out.

The proximity of his scream frightens Will, and he falls back into the fold. On his own Mason manages to crawl over and tumble into the ditch.

"Where are you hit?" a soldier asks. Will does not recognize the voice, nor can he make out the face. The fear that drove him here is fleeing, and his own pain is flooding in.

"My knee. Oh, God. Will? Will?"

He scrambles forward and lifts Mason's head to his lap. The rifle fire continues with renewed vigour.

"Will?"

"Yeah. It's me." His voice is a coarse croak. His throat burns.

"Oh, Jesus, it hurts, Will." Mason's voice is calmer now. It's possible that he is crying, but Will can't be sure in the dark.

"Christ," says the soldier from earlier. He is staring at Mason's open wound.

"Shut up," Will hisses.

"It's bad, isn't it? Is it bad?"

"Mason," Will whispers in his friend's ear. "You have to be quiet, okay? We've got to be near the laager here. If they find us before dawn ..." Will's voice trails off, his energy bleeding away, but Mason remains quiet. A soft whimpering now and then. A sniffle.

"What if we can't get out of here?" says Wilson.

"We've got to dig in."

"Hey. Who goes there?" Another soldier further south raises his rifle. Several others prepare to fire.

"Don't shoot," a British voice returns.

A company of sappers leaps over the ridge. Many have shovels, a few picks. Will determines their numbers to be almost seventy-five between the two groups.

"I think we're above the laager," says the unit sergeant. "If we dig in here, we might well have a jump on them in the morning."

Mason is stowed with the other wounded. Several times he cries out as they shift him down the ridge. The men begin to dig with picks. The gun battle slows to random fire again, and Will notices that the noise of their labour draws a few shots.

"We must be close," he says.

"Yeah," says the sergeant next to him. "But those shells are sailing high. Hey, you all right?"

Will nods, raises his hand.

"Nah. You shove off down the line with that other bloke. Leave the digging to us." The sergeant unbuttons his holster and passes the pistol to Will. "Take this."

Unable to hold a shovel properly, Will retreats to where Mason has been laid. The moon is up, and he can see that his friend's face is bled pale. When Will elevates the injured leg, Mason does not react. He has passed out from the pain. It is better this way, thinks Will.

With the onset of morning, their strategic advantage becomes evident. A half-mile of Boer trench curves before them. The laager lies at their feet.

Down river, Will spies a dark balloon floating above the veldt and then closes his eyes.

‡

Campbell observes the scene of last night's battle. Word of the partial British retreat made it back to Command, but reports are spotty. Rifle fire splashes sporadically in the half-light. The horizon burns like a bush fire. Sunrise. It never fails to awe him.

New bodies are scattered across the veldt. Though not as many as one would have expected. It's no Magersfontein.

Cronje has extended his sniper fire. Campbell can see their rifles pop like flash bulbs. Close, he thinks. Then the big man hawks and spits over the edge of his basket.

"Take that," he says.

Campbell decides to put more space between himself and the hidden Boer gunmen, but something catches his eye. He squints down at the laager. "Would you look at that," he wonders aloud. A small company of men have dug in above Cronje's wagons.

Campbell is still calculating the consequences of this latest development, when something strikes the floor of his basket. He looks at his feet. A hole, the size of two fingers, has been opened in the wicker weft.

"Bugger me," he says quietly.

The next shell passes up through the floor and into his great stomach. The sun lifts its wings over the veldt in a fiery arc.

"Bugger me."

‡

A Boer soldier walks lazily toward the river, dragging his feet. He is young. Clean-shaven with a fop hat tipped cockily over one eye. Will is so close to him, he could spit and hit him. The commando bends at the knees and fills his canteen. At first glance, he does not appear to be carrying a weapon, though he does sport a full bandolier. The advantage of Will's position is now fully apparent. Will and the others wait only for the full light of sun.

Unfortunately, the boy turns quickly, drawn perhaps by a sound from the trench. Will meets his gaze. The Boer drops his canteen and reaches into his belt. Will fumbles with his own pistol, and they fire simultaneously. In their haste, both miss.

Will can only imagine the boy's fear as heads peek up all along the trench line. He turns, still holding the revolver in his right hand, preparing a second shot over his shoulder. That's when Will drops him. The sun flexes like a winged phoenix then, and the company opens fire into the laager all at once.

Within minutes, white flags and bed-sheets flap over the flat ground. Handkerchiefs wave from the trenches.

‡

The laager is a wasteland. Will bears witness to the devastation. Ten days under siege, and little remains of Cronje's convoy. Its mad flight north to the Modder and safety. Will covers his face with a rag to protect himself from the toxic fumes rising off the swollen carcasses of horse and mule. The accumulation of human detritus. A two-mile stretch of veldt is strewn with the waste matter of five thousand lives. He can barely see through the swarms of flies, and yet he is compelled to collect the details. Like an archaeologist he wishes to piece together the story of their passage. An overturned coffee pot. A pair of unharmed galoshes. Stray pans and kitchen utensils. A raped umbrella, open like a skeletal wing. Chests and suitcases, charred with soot and spilling humble wardrobes. Treasures reclaimed from the burnt-out bulwarks of covered wagons. Cracked wheels and shattered spokes. Garbage. Empty meat tins. Sheaves of paper flit through the camp like lost souls. Plot fragments of a ruined narrative.

And the people. He was detailed with the other members of A Company to retrieve their weapons. So many burghers rose from the earth, he thought they had awakened the dead. A long line of ragged men formed, expecting food. Tall, gaunt, rakish men with darkened eyes and long untrimmed beards. Farmers in characteristic fop hats and ill-fitting trousers. Many wore woollen vests beneath their jackets. Threadbare in some cases. A few sported ties. If Will did not know better, he'd have sworn they came directly from a humble church. A possibility supported by those who carried Bibles in their hands, their pockets.

Some packed their clay pipes and smoked while they waited. The smell of them was horrendous. Enough to rival the bloated animal cadavers. And yet, they had endured, thought Will. Held an empire at bay for ten whole days. Longer, if he considered the month-long chase over the Transvaal.

Before he entered the laager, Will saw to Mason's removal. His friend was wraith-like with blood loss. But he was alive. The knee obviously ruined. A fact Will is unable to face even now as he contemplates their achievement. The Boer surrender. The shock of Mason's maiming is equalled only by Will's discovery of the women and children of the laager. Tough and frightened, they had survived the relentless artillery pounding—the concussive destruction of lyddite shelling that erased their livestock and obliterated their possessions— by taking refuge in a series of natural caves along the river. Surfacing from their captivity in the darkness, they blinked and marched haphazardly to their men. Their sunken fathers.

Will watches them as they sit cross-legged and reunited, eating hungrily and silently the thick British porridge. He detects no shame among them. Not for their ragged appearance. Not in their surrender.

And Will feels no elation in their defeat.

Miraculously, there are fewer than three hundred Boer casualties. The cost is ten times that among the British and colonial troops.

Wilson approaches him across the field, bearing food. Will had not felt hunger until the man's arrival, but suddenly he is ravenous.

Without thinking twice, Will joins the collection of burghers. Wilson looks on a moment, and then follows Will's lead. The two men eat quietly. The Boer pay them no heed.

6

Jacobsdal

February 28, 1900

195

*S*iphokazi has vanished. Will predicted as much when the news of Campbell's death reached him. It was Barrett who revealed the loss to him. The man was weeping and was, Will suspects, actually sober. Initially, he thought, by choice. But Siphokazi's disappearance opens another possibility.

"A giant among men," he sobbed. "Bloody disgrace."

The world is changed. Will accepts that, and the knowledge of Campbell's death. Robert's words about transformation and the passage of time resonate for him now.

Will wishes that he had had the opportunity to express his condolences to the Xhosa woman, but he imagines this would have meant little to her. Historically, her husband's death is nothing more than another invasion. One more footprint on her culture, and her country, where a steady path has already been worn by Europeans. For the woman personally, Campbell's death marks her more deeply than a stranger, like Will, could ever fathom. His insignificant remarks would only magnify her loss.

He hopes that she is able to withdraw from this cataclysm and live out her life without touching the war again. But Will knows that is unlikely to happen. This war, if it is about anything, is about building roadways through the desert, gaining access to the riches beneath the sand.

He shoulders his pack, hand bandaged, face stitched, and joins the march back to Jacobsdal.

‡

Mason is asleep. It is for the best. Beneath the fresh white sheets, he sweats. But this time not from fever, or sunstroke. He dreams incalculable dreams. Although Claire imagines, somewhat melodramatically, that he dreams of running. Mason lies still as the capitol of a tomb. He gleams even in the shadows of the church hall.

Whatever he dreams, Claire is sure that his self-projection is that of someone whole and unscarred. He is, as yet, unaware of his truncated self.

When he awakens, the discovery will be cruel. He will feel nothing, physically. But his eyes will perceive the loss. The cool white sheets, laundered and smooth. And then he will look beneath, his senses confused. Some would do it slowly, hoping against all odds. But Mason will snatch away the cover, incredulous and angry.

Claire cannot be there when it happens, and so she elects to change wards. It is the worst thing she has ever done. And her guilt runs deep.

Outside the little church, the pretension of its spire bathes her in shadow. Protected, or hidden. She cannot decide.

"Hey." The voice behind her is unmistakably Hilde's.

"Hey."

The little nurse knows her too well. "It will be terrible at first. But he's alive, Claire. He'll get over it."

"No," she says with certainty. "He won't. Some people don't."

"Some people do."

"Not him."

The sun is bright white. But Claire can smell the coming rain. She walks.

"Talk to me, Claire," says Hilde.

But she is not able to. She wants to say that she switched sides partway through. She backed a winner. But that's selfish. And not entirely true. So she keeps it to herself. Because it feels better to hurt. To shoulder a burden so insignificant in comparison to his and pretend to herself it is otherwise.

Her illusions of South Africa were just as grand as Mason's. She knows this now. He will carry his illusions with him like a coat. They will keep him warm, perhaps, while she has nothing.

Uncle John,

By the time you receive this letter, you will have already read about our great victory. You will have been offered stories of our bravery and our valour in the papers. I know soldiers who believe them. But it's all rot. All of it. You said so yourself, before we left.

Anyone who's honest will tell you, we acted out of necessity. We did our jobs, if we were able—and many of us were—but we were all frightened.

If putting one foot in front of the other is valorous, then fine; we were valorous. If risking your life is courageous, then fine; we were courageous. But it's still all rot.

I've got my eyes open now. Tell that to Mason when you see him. We have to help him understand. I don't think to write again.

Yours,
Will

P.S—Please keep the enclosed letters in a safe place. They were written by a good friend.

‡

"I'm not going home," he tells her. "I'm moving north to build snow-men for a living."

Claire smiles.

They are walking on the outskirts of town where the Canadian division is mustering for its march. A light mist falls. In the distance, there is thunder.

"What about you?" The medical corps is moving to Pietermaritz-burg. Claire has been ordered to Fort Napier Medical Hospital to join other members of the Victorian Nurses. "Moving back to your father's?"

"No," she says. And it comes out more vehemently than she expected. In fact, she has not considered any of her options seriously. "The city," she answers. "Melbourne, possibly. Maybe Canberra." The life takes on the shape of truth as she speaks. A flat of her own. A quiet anonymous existence. But not as a nurse. "To teach," she says, though it has never occurred to her before now. "No snow in Victoria, I'm afraid."

Will's turn to smile. No illusions.

"What will you do really?" she asks.

"Just have a look around, I guess." The rain is falling in earnest now, but slowly, in large drops. They walk on in silence.

"When I was in school, I read about an American expedition to the North Pole ... about a man named Charles Francis Hall. That would be something. To go to the North Pole."

Claire pictures him wrapped in fur. A beard thick about his chin. Icicles hanging like stalactites. A face gone crystal.

"Yes," she says. "That would be something."

Claire reaches up to kiss him on the cheek, where the stitches are fresh and red. And then he turns. He turns and walks off towards Bloemfontein. Toward Pretoria. Dreaming of snow.

Acknowledgements

Caroline Bergeron, Donna Sorfleet, Bill Hanna, and his late wife Frances were all instrumental in seeing this book through to fruition. I thank them greatly.

Thank you to Sharon Caseburg, Jamis Paulson, and the staff at Turnstone, past and present, for their continued faith in my writing—most especially my editor, Wayne Tefs, for his insight and expertise. I would also like to thank the staff at the George Metcalf Archival Collection in the Canadian War Museum; in particular, Carol Reid and Catherine Woodcock, for their help in locating materials during my research there.

Information about the Anglo-Boer War in South Africa was drawn from *Our little army in the field: the Canadians in South Africa, 1899–1902*, by Brian A. Reid; *With The Royal Canadians*, by Stanley McKeown Brown; and *The Great Boer War*, by Sir Arthur Conan Doyle.

Also helpful were the personal scrapbooks of Colonel Oscar Charles Casgrain Pelletier and General William Dillon Otter; the correspondence of Privates Murray Hendric and Tom Snider, as well as that of Lt.-Colonel John Henry Kaye. An extensive compendium of stereoscopic images in the George Metcalf Archival Collection was also consulted.

I owe the title to my father.

Finally, the Ontario Arts Council provided generous support during the writing of this novel, in the form of a Works-in-Progress Grant, for which I am grateful.

2 - 33
3 - 51
4 - 131
5 - 161
6 - 195